SAFE
HARBOR

SAFE HARBOR

A Story of New Love

The Adventures of the Angel Oleo
Book Three

DR. AUDREY J. LEVY

PACIFIC STYLE BOOKS

www.audreylevy.com
audrey@audreylevy.com

Pacific Style Books
P.O. Box 10358
Marina Del Rey, CA 90295

Pacific Style Books are available at special discounts for bulk purchases, sales promotion, fund-raising, or educational purposes. Special editions can be created to specifications. For details, contact Special Sales Department, Pacific Style Publishers, P.O. Box 10358, Marina Del Rey, CA 90295.

ISBN 978-1-951867-03-4

Printed in the United States of America

First Edition—December 2019

Cover and interior design by Frame25 Production
Cover photos by LilKar, Garry L., and TebNad,
all c/o Shutterstock.com

For
Barbra Streisand, Kevin Costner, Nick Nolte
and
Julia Roberts

Preface

Dear Reader,

"The Adventures of Oleo" has taken on a life of her own.

The Angel Oleo has become a star in her own right. I am, apparently, merely taking dictation. A Rabbi I once knew called this "automatic writing," and the concept scared the bejeezus out of me because I thought all the "spiritual stuff" and the "psychic stuff" was bull poop.

My Dad, Albert Levy, was an atheist—as was my mentor, Dr. Eugene Landy, and my live-in companion, Dr. James Spencer. I played around with a Ouija Board in college and had a really scary experience with a friend named "Zubie" who I heard died a number of years ago. Zubie had the ability to bring "demons" through the Ouija Board, and that was enough for us to throw that board away!

I honestly don't know what to make of all the "stuff" that is coming out of my brain. I seem to be pretty prolific, even articulate, in my humble opinion. In this lifetime, I've been given blonde hair, blue eyes, and at this late stage in my life (about to turn 66 years old in December 2019), a pretty fit body for an old broad.

So, I fit the criteria to be in front of the media. The rest of my future is yet to unfold.

The book you are about to read was originally written in 1991 WITHOUT the Angel Oleo, and the main female character was named "Glenda" after "Glenda the Good Witch" in the "Wizard of Oz." I wrote it in screenplay format and it was called "Slay Ride" because my screenplay agent, at the time, said "they" were looking for "thrillers."

In order not to bore with you with a lot of unnecessary details, suffice it to say, that when I originally self-published, *Noelle's Ark* in 2008, I had no idea that *The Adventures of Oleo* was going to come into being. A very kind and wise man, Robert Friedman, who published *Conversations with God*, read my first draft, which included the book you are about to read as its second half.

Mr. Friedman said that since "Slay Ride" involved the Angel Oleo with the Mafia (!), it seemed like a "B Movie," compared to the first half of *Noelle's Ark* which he thought was "really something substantial." He suggested that I continue writing in the autobiographical fiction mode, and thus came my more personal story about my breach with my family (originally called "No Matter What" and that's what made it into the final published novel, *Noelle's Ark.*

This "Good Fellas" meets "The Miracle Worker" screenplay got put into a drawer and has resurfaced thanks to Oleo's persistence in my brain! We both think that, regardless of it seeming like a "B Movie," it remains quite funny and entertaining. Therefore, Oleo and I bring you back to the characters of Noelle and Jimmy Splendor in the renamed *Safe Harbor* novella.

Oleo, any comments?

Of course!

I beseech Hollywood and the rest of the world to make "The Adventures of Oleo" into popcorn movies and a family television series to fight the war against the Dark Side that is trying to destroy the very foundation of our civilization—"family." All of our cultures depend on the "family" as the basic building block for our strength. The "Me Too" movement, the fight against racism, the fight to end poverty and famine—all of our moral dilemmas—the root of these moral dilemmas comes down to our denial of taking responsibility for our own actions.

Most of us depend on the "other guy" to take care of all "those problems." Well, guess what? The buck really does stop here. We—I—need to take responsibility for my own ripple effect.

Patrick Henry, one of the Founding Fathers of the United States and currently an angel, is who said, "Give me liberty, or give me death." His influence helped create the Bill of Rights, which guaranteed personal freedoms and set limits on the government's power. He also said, "United we Stand, divided we fall."

The Dark Side does indeed exist and it can permeate the souls of even our most brilliant people. Its Force is dividing us. Our family structure is being eaten away by our various dysfunctional behaviors, which prevent us from having healthy households and becoming healthy adults.

Humans need to hold predators and those who condone predatory behavior accountable for their actions. It starts at home in our own families. The alpha parent cannot be allowed to abuse and exploit minor children while the other parent watches, or worse yet, provokes the irrational outbursts. We need to use positive reinforcement instead of punishment to change the world. The rampant rise of domestic abuse and the rate of suicide, especially among teenagers, is exponentially rising. Drug addicts, alcoholics, sex addicts, gamblers, murderers, warmongers, and people with no conscience are in positions of great power.

It may seem trite to repeat a Beatles lyric, but "All we need is love . . . ."

HUMANS MUST LOVE EACH OTHER AND ALL LIVING THINGS UNCONDITIONALLY TO ACHIEVE WORLD PEACE . . . ACCEPTANCE AND FORGIVENESS ARE THE KEYS TO HEALING!

It may also seem trite to repeat the words of Mr. George Lucas, but "May the Force be with you . . . ."

With lots and lots and LOTS of love,

Oleo

Prologue

To recap—In *Noelle's Ark*, Jimmy Splendor was an atheist. When he woke up in Heaven, he didn't believe he was dead and he certainly didn't believe he was in Heaven. Greeted by his father, whom he hated on Earth, Jimmy took off running for seven years Earth time (only a few minutes in Heaven). He finally met an angel named Oleo, who encouraged him to help his former wife, Noelle, who was still having nightmares years after Jimmy's passing.

Jimmy and Oleo visited Noelle in her dreams and stimulated her to write a book about her life in order to purge her emotional baggage. Through the method of written conversations with the angels of her loved ones, including her parents, Noelle was able to use the process of writing as a means of examining and dealing with the most painful episodes of her life.

As her nightmares faded, and she began to find peace, Jimmy encouraged Noelle to fantasize about falling in love again. He tells her to write a new life script for herself that has a happy ending instead of her actual truly tragic life in which she was disinherited by her parents, lost the respect of her brothers, and the love of her life died at the tender age of 56 from the disease of alcoholism, leaving her in debt, alone, and suicidal.

Noelle responded by speaking to the angel in her mind that she called Jimmy.

And just how do you propose I accomplish this amazing feat, my love, of fantasizing about falling in love again.

By writing your new life script, of course.

Of course. Shall I start at any particular place?

Guess where.

The Beginning.

Yes, but make it "The New Beginning."

All right, but honey—

Yes.

Since we're only playing pretend, let's make it an alcoholic that gets sober this time around.

Okay, if you like.

And someone who's kind with a great sense of humor, can carry his own weight financially, and who loves dogs and loves sex.

With dogs or humans?

Smart ass.

Couldn't resist. Let your imagination rule. It's your book.

Our book.

We're all one.

Right. I keep forgetting. Anyway, we need to get to know him first. What he's like before I come into the picture. Somebody totally new and different . . .

Let your mind wander . . . No restrictions . . .

"Do not let your fire go out, spark by irre-placeable spark in the hopeless swamps of the not-quite, the not-yet, and the not-at-all. Do not let the hero in your soul perish in lonely frustration for the life you deserved and have never been able to reach. The world you desire can be won.

It exists . . . it is real . . . it is possible."

—Ayn Rand

1

The New Beginning

CENTRAL PARK at night was filled with hard packed white snow. It was Christmas Eve in New York City, and a Santa Claus prepared his sleigh. Only this Santa packed a butcher knife, his blade gleaming in the moonlight.

Suddenly, he slashed the head off a topiary elephant. Santa's eyes twinkled . . .

Outside the park, at a parking meter, a car rocked from side to side. Inside the car, a couple, half-naked, fucked in the front seat. The man said, "Let's go dancing, Suzy Q."

Suzy Q said, "I thought you didn't know how."

The man replied, "Hell, I met you in a nightclub!"

Suzy Q snickered. "But you just went there to get drunk, hit on girls, and get into fights!"

The man brought his shoulders up proudly. "Well, that's dancing, Suzy Q!"

Back in Central Park, Santa was ready to dance. He rode his sleigh. Sang his own carol.

Santa bellowed, "Slashing through the snow, In a one horse open sleigh, O'er the fields we go, Slashing all the way!"

Santa got into the song with gusto. He pulled out his butcher knife, using it to slice off topiary heads and trembling branches.

Santa sang, "Bells on bobtails ring, Making spirits bright. Oh what fun it is to slash and sing, A slaying song tonight!"

Outside the Central Park Social Center, our young couple from the car, headed to a crowd and banner that said, "Central Park Christmas Eve Dance."

Suzy Q saw Santa in the distance. "Look, there's Santa!"

Everyone turned to look. Suzy ran toward Santa. Santa was in his own world. He raised and lowered his gleaming butcher knife, while singing aloud.

"Bells on bobtails ring, Making spirits bright . . ."

Suzy Q ran closer.

Santa sang louder. "Oh what fun it is to slash and sing . . ."

Suzy Q was horrified to see Santa had a butcher knife.

"A SLAYING song tonight!"

Santa's knife whizzed down, decapitating the running Suzy Q. Red blood spattered against white snow.

Everyone screamed as Santa rode away.

$$\approx$$

An amusement park pulsed with life. Screams were heard from people riding the gleaming roller coaster. Jonathan Weber, a handsome 50 year old, sat next to a man, whose face was turned away from him.

Suddenly, the man stood, and tried to jump out of the moving car. Jonathan grabbed him. The man struggled desperately to jump out of the roller coaster. They reached the top of the maze.

Jonathan yelled, "Help!!"

The other people on the coaster were terrified, watching the men claw at each other. Jonathan took in all his breath to yell as loudly as he could.

"Heeeellllppp!!!"

In an elegant bedroom in Beverly Hills, Melinda Weber, Jonathan's beautiful wife, bolted up in bed. Christmas morning had arrived, and her husband was screaming for help in bed next to her. Melinda shook him awake.

"Jonathan, wake up!"

Jonathan's eyes snapped open. He was frightened and sweating. Melinda caressed his forehead.

Jonathan grimaced. "I was having a nightmare, Melly."

Melly smiled tolerantly. "I know, honey."

"A man was trying to kill himself . . . What time is it?"

"Seven. I'll make Christmas breakfast."

Jonathan was confused. "Where's the new cook?"

"Servants always get Christmas off."

"I forgot."

"Blackout."

Jonathan lovingly took Melinda in his arms. "Be nice, Melinda, and Santa will give you a special present."

Melinda saluted. "Ready, willing, and able, sir." She pulled off her pajama top, and they snuggled naked.

Jonathan nuzzled her. Melinda slid down, kissing Jonathan's chest and stomach. "Remember last Christmas, Johnny? How we giggled with that wonderful bottle of breakfast champagne?"

Jonathan tensed slightly, pulling Melinda back up. "We're sober nearly six months."

Melinda pouted. "But it's Christmas!"

Jonathan was stern, bypassing his own desire. "I don't want things to get ugly. Everybody's waiting for us to fall off the wagon. Even the kids . . ."

Melinda surrendered without anymore fight. "Okay, let's make push-push."

Jonathan laughed, and took her in his arms, hugging her tightly. "I love you, Melly."

"I love you, Johnny."

They kissed fiercely in their king sized bed, surrounded by a luxurious bedroom filled with fine art. Through their bay window was a beautiful view of their gated estate.

≈

Just down the street was parked a black limousine with New York plates and dark tinted windows.

Inside the limousine, Joey Malone sat low in the driver's seat. A .357 Magnum rested next to him.

Resting his head against the passenger window, Louie Ciccone wore dark glasses, and snored loudly. A cell phone rested on Louie's big chest. A 9mm automatic in his shoulder holster was exposed.

≈

In the Weber bedroom, just as Jonathan and Melinda were climaxing, the phone rang. Jonathan closed his eyes, and finished shuddering while the phone rang again. Then he picked up the receiver.

"Hello . . ." Jonathan listened, and his face turned into a scowl.

Melinda whispered to him in the background. "Is it your evil stepsister, Johnny? Can't Lucy give us a break on Christmas?"

Jonathan put his hand over Melinda's mouth, while he tried to listen to his caller. Melinda pushed his hand away, and stuck her tongue out at him. Suddenly, Jonathan yelled into the phone.

"I'm on vacation! Tell him to get a different criminal attorney!"

Jonathan slammed down the phone. Melinda jumped a half mile. "Did Uncle Vito refer that case?"

Jonathan dumped his anger on her. "Wives don't ask, Melinda!"

Melinda stormed to a huge closet with mirrored doors. She put on a flannel shirt, jeans, and a pair of Nikes, then stalked out.

Jonathan angrily pushed the mirrors the other way, revealing a bunch of his suits all lined up in a row. He pushed the door further open. More suits.

Jonathan quickly put on dress slacks, a sweater, and loafers, then ran after Melinda.

Jonathan entered the living room, and Melinda turned to him, all smiles. She pointed to a floor to ceiling Christmas tree, surrounded by a mountain of presents, and Billy Weber, 10, next to Jenny Weber, five.

The children ecstatically ripped open gifts as fast as their little fingers would allow them. Billy was the first to notice their parents. "You guys are late! Jenny and I have been here since dawn!"

Jonathan slipped his fingers through his belt loops, and sauntered up to Billy like John Wayne would have. "Well, Billy, you're just hot shit!"

Melinda gently put her fingers over Jonathan's mouth. "No swearing in front of the kids! And I can't stay mad at you, when I see how generous you are!"

Jonathan smiled as Melinda hugged him tightly. Jenny, holding a teddy bear almost bigger than she was, ran up to their legs.

"Santa left a 1000 presents!"

Jonathan lifted the laughing child high into the air. "How's my sunshine this morning?"

"I love you, Daddy!"

Billy opened another package. He pulled out a Batman costume. "Cool! I can be Batman!" He sang the theme. "Dada dada . . . Batman!!"

Jenny ran back to watch Billy unfold the outfit. Jonathan extended his hand to Billy. "Let me see the mask."

Billy threw Jonathan Batman's mask, and Jonathan put it on, dancing around the room, and singing.

"Dada dada . . . Batman!!"

Jonathan's family howled with laughter. Jonathan grabbed Melinda, swinging her with him. She good-naturedly tried to escape.

"I've got to start breakfast!"

Jonathan swung her through the air. "Not until we open our presents!"

Jenny yelled, "Yay!"

Sounding important, Billy said, "The milk's sour, Mom."

Melinda's smile changed to a frown. "Damn, I'll go to the store."

Jonathan wagged his index finger. "No swearing in front of the kids! C'mon, I'll drive you."

Jonathan pretended to fly out of the living room. As Billy and Jenny laughed, Melinda stopped him, pulling off the Batman mask.

"Not as Batman, you won't!"

In the black limousine, Louie snored, and Joey smoked. The phone rang, causing them both to jump. The phone fell off Louie's chest, and he clumsily grabbed it, his stubby fingers trying to open the compact instrument.

"Yeah . . . Hello . . . okay."

Louie disconnected the line, and turned to Joey. "We do it, Joey."

Joey nodded grimly. "I hope the boss knows what's goin' on here, Louie, cuz I sure don't."

Louie shook his head, worried. "Uncle Vito always says, 'Watch your back, kid.'"

≈

Jonathan and Melinda got into a teal Mercedes parked in their driveway next to a cream Rolls Royce and a silver Rolls Royce. As they adjusted their seat belts, Jonathan spoke first.

"Melly, I'm sorry about before, and I will tell you this much."

Melinda tilted her head, her eyes frightened. She listened without comment.

Jonathan swallowed hard. "A cousin of my father's first wife did Uncle Vito a favor.

He went to Central Park, dressed up as Santa Claus, and cut off a specific woman's head!"

Melinda's eyebrows raised. "That's Lucy's side of the family!"

"Yes. My father and Uncle Vito want a relative, other than Lucy, to defend him instead of an East Coast shark."

Melinda sniffed disbelievingly. "They want you, because you're the best lawyer they know!"

Jonathan laughed modestly. "You're biased." He started the car's motor. Melinda turned it off, and put her other hand on Jonathan's arm.

"Uncle Vito referred the case. Maybe you should take it, so he doesn't get angry."

"But I'm on vacation!" Jonathan protested.

Melinda shrugged her shoulders. "My father works on vacation if Uncle Vito calls. When I asked him why, he said, you don't want to fuck with the dragon . . . and my father's a senator!"

Melinda laughed nervously, but Jonathan got angry. "I'm sick of the goddamn family! We're both alcoholics because of the family!"

Melinda shook her head. "No. We can't blame them! In rehab, they told us we couldn't blame anyone but ourselves."

"I don't care what they told us in rehab! Those doctors don't know our family! I'm glad I left that hospital. You stayed, and you wanted champagne with breakfast!"

"You're just too conservative, Johnny. Look at you, wearing dress slacks on Christmas! You won't even let me buy you a pair of jeans!"

Jonathan shook his head ruefully. "Uncle Vito says they're inappropriate for a *consigliere*."

Melinda got the shivers. "He is so weird! And Lucy is, too. I swear she hates us for getting married."

"C'mon, Melly, don't start that again. Lucy was only 10 years old when she wanted to marry me. And I was five!"

"Hell hath no fury like a woman scorned. She tried to kill you when you were seven!"

Jonathan shook his head. "I don't think she realized the severity of what she was doing."

"Honey, once Lucy was old enough to know she wasn't related to the family by blood, the men were fair game. Especially after your Mom and Uncle Vito's wife died, Lucy was mistress of the family's universe until I came along . . . and then you abandoned her!"

Jonathan's frustration mounted. "But I talk to her every damn day!"

"And you hate it!" Melinda emphasized.

Jonathan banged his fist against the steering wheel. "Shit . . . I do hate this crap!"

Melinda slumped down in her seat. "I wish we could really fly away . . ."

Jonathan started the motor, and pushed the gate opener button. "You want to fly? Let's fly!"

≈

The estate's gates cranked open. Jonathan and Melinda careened out. In the black limousine, Joey jumped into action, jamming the limo into gear to follow the Benz. Louie was thrown forward, and he cursed loudly.

Jonathan raced through the canyon with Melinda laughing like a teenager. Behind them, the limo's brakes screamed around turns.

Jonathan suddenly screeched into a parking space across the street from a Mom and Pop market. He and Melinda beamed at each other. She threw her arms around him. "Just like the old days, Johnny!"

They got out of the car, and clasped hands to cross the street. Without warning, the speeding limousine nearly mowed them down, but they jumped back, falling against the Benz.

Melinda screamed, and Jonathan kicked the car, which was roaring away, its New York license plates disappearing around a curve.

Jonathan yelled at the swirling dust. "Fucking New Yorkers can't drive! You almost fucking killed us!"

When Jonathan and Melinda returned home, Billy and Jenny greeted them in the entry hall. Billy said, "Aunt Lucy called. She said, Uncle Vito wants us to come for lunch instead of dinner, cuz he has to go to New York."

Jonathan's shoulders drooped. "Melinda, why do we have to go there for Christmas every year?"

Melinda's eyes registered resignation. "Uncle Vito wants it that way . . ."

In the driveway, Melinda sat behind the wheel of the cream Rolls Royce, motor running. Billy was next to her. Jonathan and Jenny walked out of the house, holding hands. They got into the back seat.

Jenny slid over behind her mother, who pushed a button for the gate. Melinda inched out of the driveway. Her view was blocked by a dumpster parked a few feet away that wasn't there before.

Melinda was annoyed. "Who left that dumpster there?"

Jonathan pondered this. Jenny stuck her head out the window. "I'll see if I can see, Mommy."

Melinda darted the car out into the street. Jonathan did a double take, suddenly realizing . . . "Jenny, get your head back in here!"

Too late. The Rolls was hit by a thundering semi tractor that took the passenger car out like it was cardboard. Hit and run.

≈

2

In the emergency room, Jonathan, covered with blood, was wheeled in on a stretcher. A doctor and two orderlies struggled to keep him down.

". . . Why won't you bastards tell me what happened to my wife and kids?! Where's my baby, Jenny?!"

"Please, Mr. Weber. Be calm." The doctor prepared a shot while the orderlies held Jonathan.

"No! Get away from me! Somebody's trying to kill me!!" Jonathan tried to jump out of the way. The orderlies restrained him, and the doctor approached, needle extended.

"Nobody's trying to kill you . . ."

"But they are! The limo was . . ."

The doctor jammed the needle into Jonathan's vein. Jonathan jumped, but immediately relaxed. He spoke softly and slowly.

"It . . . it had . . . New York plates . . ."

The doctor spoke soothingly. "Your father and sister are here."

Jonathan jumped, protesting through his haze. "No! No! Keep them . . . away! Don't you get it?! My family . . . my family . . . is *the* family!"

~

A black limousine, leading a funeral procession, parked, as did other cars. The Chauffeur got out, turned, and his identity was revealed as Joey Malone.

Joey formally opened the passenger door. Billy exited first, his head wrapped in a bandage, face bruised. Joey waited a moment, then leaned in, and almost lifted Jonathan out.

Jonathan, dazed and confused, used a cane to propel himself out of the limo. Behind Jonathan, a woman's hand pushed him out toward Joey. As she emerged, a black hat with a wide brim covered her features and her hair in a tight bun.

The woman, Lucy Weber, stepped out of the car, lifting her impassive face to the mourners. Lucy turned to help her father, Martin Weber, out of the back seat.

Martin's older bones moved slowly. Everyone walked together to the graveside. On his way to the eulogy, Martin clasped hands with Senator Hugh Kohler.

"Hugh, we are all so sad . . ."

The Senator nodded, his eyes watery. He hugged Jonathan, Billy, and Lucy, who sat next to him in the first row.

Jonathan stared into the distance. Dull, red eyes.

Billy glared at the double graves.

Lucy sat ramrod straight. In control. She listened to Martin speak.

"I am Martin Weber. Melinda's father-in-law. Jenny's grandfather. I am in great pain today. I know that Melinda's father, Senator Hugh Kohler, is also devastated at this loss . . ."

Martin suddenly stopped talking, as his eyes caught sight of someone arriving for the services. Jonathan turned to see who his father was looking at.

Vito Ciccone worked his way through the crowd, which seemed to part for him. His nephew Louie walked behind him, nodding somberly to people.

People craned their necks to see the impeccably dressed Vito, his body thick and powerful. A diamond ring glittered on his pinkie. Vito indicated with a bow of his head for Martin to continue.

Mourners arrived from the funeral, parking their cars outside Jonathan's house. Inside, a maid, Inga, served guests at a buffet table.

Billy ran through the dining room into the living room with children following him like he was the Pied Piper.

They passed by a remote camera lens and microphone hidden in a plant.

Inside a small surveillance room, several television monitors, displaying the rooms of the house, were observed by Vito, Martin, Lucy, and Louie.

Watching the living room, they saw the butler, Manny, mixing drinks at the bar. Jonathan stumbled in, cane wobbling.

Billy tried to help him balance, but Jonathan shook him off. Others stepped out of his way as he headed to the bar. Reaching it, he mumbled to Manny. "Line 'em up, Manny. Fast!"

Vito immediately alerted. "Uh oh . . . Louie, go get Jonathan outta there!"

In the living room, Manny lined up three shot glasses, pouring vodka into each one. Jonathan downed the first. Just as he was about to take the second, an arm stopped him.

Louie spoke in a low tone. "C'mon, Johnny, Lucy's makin' a place for you to lie down."

Jonathan spoke loudly. "I bet. It's my house. Get your fucking hands offa me."

The people standing with Senator Kohler gasped and whispered.

Inside the surveillance room, Vito, Martin, and Lucy watched Louie on their television screen. He looked at the crowd self-consciously, while Billy addressed his friends.

"C'mon, guys. This is the part when my old man shows what an asshole he can be."

Billy led his troop out of the living room. Jonathan downed the second shot, and reached for the third.

Vito nudged Lucy. "Lucy, go help Louie!"

In the living room, Louie touched Jonathan's arm again. Jonathan swung at him.

"Get offa me, you goon!"

Louie ducked. Jonathan almost fell, but Louie caught him. Suddenly, Lucy's stern voice was heard.

"Jonathan, dear . . ."

Everybody turned. Lucy walked in, speaking softly but firmly.

"Jonathan, let Louie help you."

"Fuck Big Louie, and you too!" Jonathan said, more than loudly.

Lucy straightened her shoulders, and stretched her neck. "Father isn't going to like this."

"Fuck him, too, and stop bein' his mouthpiece, Lucy!" Jonathan again reached for the third shot.

Lucy nodded to Louie. Before Jonathan could drink, Louie grabbed his wrist, and twisted Jonathan's arm up behind his back. The cane fell.

Jonathan yelled in pain, struggling to get away. People watched surreptitiously.

In the surveillance room, Vito wheeled on Martin.

"Martin, your adult children are acting like idiots!"

Louie tried to lead a rebellious Jonathan out of the living room past the stunned observers. Suddenly, Martin appeared.

"What are you doing?!"

Martin removed Louie's grip from Jonathan's arm. Jonathan backed away, bobbing and weaving, dragging his bad leg. With great bravado, he addressed Louie.

"C'mon, mother fucker! Let's go!"

Louie looked at Lucy for instructions. She looked at Martin, who stared at her reprovingly. He turned to the guests.

"Please excuse my son on this tragic day of losing his wife and daughter."

Martin tried to lead Jonathan and Lucy from the room. Jonathan kept swinging at Louie. Louie blocked the blows, and Jonathan tripped.

Suddenly, Vito entered to see Jonathan sitting flat on his ass. Vito's eyes flickered angrily, but recovering his composure, he nodded to Louie, who lifted Jonathan, practically carrying the broken man from the room. Jonathan wanted the last word.

"I'll get ya, Big Louie . . ."

Vito nodded to Martin and Lucy to exit with him.

The three dark figures entered the library. Lucy went to the bar. Vito and Martin proceeded to the small surveillance room off the library.

Once inside, they sat in front of the mute TV monitors. Martin shifted nervously, waiting for Vito to speak first.

"Martin, you'll have to apologize personally to Senator Kohler."

"Of course, Vito."

Lucy brought drinks to the two men, retreating to the shadows. Martin noticed her lingering.

"Lucy, leave us alone, please."

Lucy was hurt, but didn't let the men see.

"All right, Father."

She headed for the door, leaving it the slightest bit ajar when she exited. There was a beat of silence between the two men.

This time Martin spoke first. "I apologize for my son, Vito."

"It's good enough for Senator Kohler, but this is Vito Ciccone you're talkin' to. I ought to have that son of yours whacked!"

"But he's your blood, too, Vito! Billy would be an orphan!"

"Nobody in the family is an orphan! When you married my sister 55 years ago, and brought Lucy with you, I didn't say no, did I?"

"No, Vito. I appreciate how generous you have been, and . . ."

"Shut up, Martin!"

Martin cringed, his eyes flashing a mixture of anger and fear. Vito abruptly stood, walking to the library. Martin followed.

Lucy's ear was listening at the library door to the surveillance room. She flew across the room, shutting the library door behind her, but left it the slightest bit ajar as well.

Vito and Martin entered. Vito went to the bar. Martin sat on the edge of an antique chair in front of a marble fireplace.

"Martin, Lucy was five years old, deserted by her mother. When you tried to bullshit me about where your first wife had gone, I found out the truth, didn't I?"

"Yes, Vito."

"Even though you told me the bitch had run away, I found out she got the electric chair for whackin' some poor bastard, didn't I?"

"Yes, Vito."

Vito moved to stand threateningly over Martin. "So after all these years of my generosity, why would you still try to bullshit me?"

"We've worked so hard to groom Jonathan to be my successor that I thought . . ."

Vito cut him off. "You didn't think! His behavior was out of control long before this car accident. I've had Lucy updating me since he and Melinda went to that rehab hospital. Jonathan hasn't stayed sober for a full six months. He is embarrassing the family! We have to eliminate embarrassments!!"

"Please, Vito. Let me talk to him. Give Jonathan some more time."

"That's what you said before he went into the hospital! What if the FBI approaches him when he's out drunk somewhere? It may have already happened!"

Martin stood to protest vehemently. "No! Jonathan is loyal!"

Vito softened. He put his hand on Martin's shoulder.

"He learned that from you, Martin. You were loyal to my sister, and you have been loyal to me. If I thought otherwise, I would not have made you *consigliere*."

Martin went to the fireplace, using the poker to stir ashes. "I never forgave myself for her suicide."

Vito shrugged his shoulders. "If my sister shootin' herself was your fault, I'd have personally taken you out. She wasn't cut out for this life. She never even liked fishing. Cried if my father or I killed a fish to eat."

Martin said sadly, "If only we'd let her go to start somewhere new . . ."

"There's no escape, Martin. She knew too many secrets. So does Jonathan. Either he shapes up or we ship him out in cement shoes."

"But, Vito, who would succeed me as *consigliere*?"

Vito sighed deeply. "I'm thinkin' about Lucy."

"A woman?! Chicago won't approve!"

Vito angrily poked his finger into Martin's shoulder. "You tellin' me I need your permission?!"

"Of course not, Vito!"

Vito backed off Martin by a few inches. "If somethin' happens to your son, I've already told Lucy she's next in line."

"Give Jonathan six more months."

"You got one month. He's takin' the road his mother took, and I don't want to go down with him."

"You won't give the order to hurt him before that?"

Vito nodded. "You have my word."

Vito and Martin started for the doorway.

In the hallway, Lucy's ear was glued to the library door. She quickly darted into the kitchen, just as Vito and Martin came into the hallway.

≈

3

Lucy ran head on into Louie, who was munching on an apple, on his way out of the kitchen. "Oh! Louie!"

Louie put his arms around Lucy, trying to kiss her.

"It's okay, honey. I don't get to touch you enough anyway."

"Shh! Stop it!" Lucy tried to move Louie's arms off of her, while looking over his shoulder at a rotund cook, Myrna, who seemed absorbed over pots on a stove. Lucy headed through the kitchen up a back stairway.

Louie followed her up the stairs, trying to grab her tits. He whispered, "C'mon, Lucy, give us a little."

Lucy angrily pushed him away. She also whispered, "Not here, Louie! I told you, no one must know about us! Where's Jonathan?"

"Joey and me put him in bed. He took a couple of those pills the Doc left before the funeral, and fell asleep."

Lucy started further up the steps. Louie took her arm. "When do I see you again, honey?"

"I'm not sure, Louie."

"But, honey . . ."

Suddenly, Manny and Inga entered the kitchen, carrying trays. They walked past the back staircase on the way to the sink, seeing Lucy and Louie whispering.

Lucy assumed a loud formal tone. "Louie, we'll discuss it later."

Lucy retreated up the rear stairs. Louie shrugged his shoulders and went down the stairs.

As he entered the kitchen, Louie saluted Manny and Inga, and pinched Myrna's ass.

Myrna jumped. "Oh! Louie, you startled me!"

Louie laughed. "Keeps ya young, Myrna!"

After Louie walked out, Manny, Inga, and Myrna exchanged glances. "Poor Louie," Inga said.

Myrna chimed in. "Inga, that Lucy's been leading Mr. Ciccone's nephew around since they were kids, stealing cookies from my kitchen. She thinks nobody knows. Hah!"

Manny put in his two cents. "Lucy Weber is one tough bitch!"

They all laughed.

Lucy tiptoed into Jonathan's bedroom, peered at him apparently sleeping, and whispered, "Johnny, are you awake?"

Jonathan didn't stir. Lucy checked the door over her shoulder, then took a small bottle of cocaine out of her pocket. She expertly snorted a spoonful of the white powder up both nostrils.

Lucy lightly caressed Jonathan's cheek, and whispered, "Johnny, it's official. I overheard Uncle Vito telling Daddy that if something happens to you, I get to be *consigliere* when Daddy dies. Since Louie could take over for Uncle Vito, he and I would make great leaders for the family."

Lucy inhaled a couple more hits of cocaine, then returned the bottle to her pocket. She licked her fingers, and wiped her nose.

"You know, Johnny, I'd dump Louie in a second, if you would just . . . but I'm being silly. We'll take one step at a time. With Melinda gone, maybe . . ."

Lucy examined the medicine bottle on Jonathan's night table. She was counting the pills, when suddenly, Martin entered. Lucy jumped, clumsily dropping the pills back into the bottle.

"What are you doing?" Martin asked suspiciously.

Lucy regained her composure, putting the bottle on the table. "Checking to make sure Jonathan hasn't taken too many pills."

"I find it hard to believe you're worried about Jonathan."

"Father, why do you persist in questioning my motives?"

"I've told you before, dear, don't take things personally. You and Jonathan have given the term 'sibling rivalry' new meaning."

"I know he feels badly. He loved Melinda and Jenny."

"And I love you, Lucy."

Lucy lowered her eyes. "Thank you. I appreciate that you adopted me after Mother ran away."

"I'm proud you've become a successful lawyer, and I pity your opponents . . . What did you find in the pill bottle?"

"It appears he took two extra."

Martin sighed. "He'll sleep until tomorrow. I'll come back to talk to him. Let's go apologize to Senator Kohler."

Martin escorted Lucy out of the room. Jonathan opened his bloodshot eyes. He took two more pills out of the bottle, and a silver flask from under the mattress.

Jonathan swallowed the pills, and closed his eyes.

~

A few days later, Billy flew a buzzing remote controlled airplane out on the pool patio. His face was still healing. Jonathan came out, unshaven, wearing sunglasses, a robe, and using his cane.

Jonathan sat down at a table set for lunch. A rolled up *Los Angeles Times* was next to a glass of orange juice.

Billy supplied his own sound effects. "Rat-a-tat! Take that, you bastards!"

Jonathan nursed a hangover. "Enough, Billy! Headache time!"

"So what!" Billy yelled. "Brrrrrrr! Rat-a-tat!!"

Jonathan jumped up, going after Billy, who ran away, screaming, "Help! Somebody help me!"

Manny the butler ran onto the patio. He saw Jonathan throw his newspaper at Billy, but miss. Jonathan limped back to the table, huffing and puffing.

Manny bowed. "Is there something I can do, sir?"

Jonathan swallowed a gulp of orange juice, and immediately spit it back into the glass. "Yeah. Vodka in the o.j., and my newspaper. It's on the lawn."

"Very well, sir. Will that be all?"

"Find Billy. It's lunch time."

"He seems to have run away, sir."

"Well, there's only so many places he can hide, goddamn it!" Jonathan yelled.

Manny raised his eyebrows. "I wouldn't underestimate young Mr. Weber's hiding technique."

Manny retrieved the newspaper, and picked up the orange juice.

Jonathan was curious. "Have you played with Billy?"

Manny shook his head. "Not exactly, sir. His mother often had difficulty discovering his whereabouts, and frequently dispatched me to perform the task."

"You think he misses his mother?" Jonathan asked.

"I believe it has been demonstrated that no matter how, shall we say, aberrant, our mother's behavior is, the separation-individuation process is never easy."

Jonathan laughed. "In other words, we all miss Mama."

"Yes, sir."

"My wife hired an intelligent man," Jonathan said.

"Thank you, sir, but it was your sister, who hired me."

Jonathan was surprised. His brows furrowed in concern. "Why did that happen?"

"Your sister hired all the new servants in the past six months," Manny said. "It is not my place to ask why."

"Of course not," Jonathan said. "All right, Manny, how about that drink?"

Manny turned to leave, but changed his mind. "If I may, sir, I'd like to express my sympathies on the passing of Mrs. Weber and Mistress Jenny."

Jonathan nodded, swallowing his remembered pain. Manny took his leave.

〜

Still in his robe, Jonathan was asleep in the library, his body spread out on the couch next to an empty bottle of vodka, and the open newspaper.

Lucy and Martin entered. Martin tried to stir him. "Jonathan?"

Lucy picked up the overturned vodka bottle and gathered the newspaper together.

Martin tried again. "Jonathan, wake up!"

Suddenly, Jonathan sat straight up. "I didn't do anything wrong!"

"No one said you had, my boy," Martin said comfortingly.

"Where's Billy?" Lucy asked, trying to catch Jonathan doing something wrong.

Jonathan rubbed his eyes. "He's hiding."

"Apparently, so are you," she drawled.

"Bitch," Jonathan said.

"Jonathan . . ." Martin interceded.

Frustrated, Jonathan stood, started to walk to the bar, but lost his balance. Lucy handed him his cane, and Jonathan angrily took it.

"Get away from me! I don't need your help!" Jonathan hobbled to the bar, making himself a drink.

Martin cleared his throat. "Prepare for a few changes around here, Jonathan."

Jonathan took his first slug. "We've already had some pretty major changes."

Martin pressed on. "Melinda and Jenny were tragedies, but . . ."

"You're already dismissing them?!"

"I'm not dismissing them, but . . ." Martin glanced at Lucy, asking with his eyes for her to speak.

Lucy obliged him. "What Father's trying to say . . ."

"Ah, the official mouthpiece!" Jonathan growled.

Martin spoke sternly. "Jonathan, you owe Lucy some respect!"

"Bullshit! Giving up my wife and daughter on Christmas Day wiped out all my debts, and tonight's New Year's Eve. So Happy New Year, dear family!"

Jonathan toasted them, and downed his drink.

Martin started pacing. "You're talking nonsense. It's time to move forward."

"Never doubted it, Father." Jonathan poured himself another drink.

Lucy angrily ripped it from his hands. Jonathan furiously pushed her, but lost his balance, falling into a chair.

Martin roared, "You act like Billy's age instead of a multimillionaire partner in a thriving law firm!"

"Yeah, thriving off the blood of others! We're fucking vampires!!"

Lucy snorted, "You're so pale, you look like one!"

"How supportive, dear sister!"

Martin took charge. "Lucy, get Joey and Manny to make sure Jonathan dresses for dinner. Find Billy, too. We'll meet Ms. Splendor here in the library."

Jonathan was sulking. "I can't wait. Who's Ms. Splendor?"

Lucy exited, and Martin ignored Jonathan's question, making a drink for himself instead.

"You have one month to change your act. Vito said he won't order you hurt before that."

"And you believed him?" Jonathan asked incredulously.

"He gave me his word," Martin said solemnly.

Jonathan took this in, and then suddenly blurted out, "Melinda and Jenny dying wasn't an accident!"

Martin did a double take, and Jonathan continued. "The only accident was that Billy and I survived!"

Martin was very troubled. "Why do you think that?"

"A limo with New York plates tried to run us down that morning."

This wasn't good enough for Martin. "You've built a steady trail of enemies. I say we give Vito the benefit of the doubt."

Jonathan smirked. "What a surprise . . . Who's this Ms. Splendor anyway?"

"She'll introduce herself."

~

Well, honey, what do you think? You like it?

I wish you could see me smiling and hear me laughing.

Whats so funny?

The Mafia, Noelle? You want your new love to be in the Mob?

Well, no, but ... this is a book, and books are supposed to be exciting, and you told me to let my mind wander ... No restrictions ...

Indeed I did, and he certainly is an alcoholic in need of sobriety, is capable of kindness, knows how to laugh, can carry his own weight financially, and appears to enjoy sex. I can't tell if he loves dogs yet.

Oh yes, that reminds me, in the story, I've decided to be a teacher instead of a psychologist, so that I'm not restricted by ethical considerations when I fall in love.

Mm hmm. Anything else?

Yes. I've moved myself to a little place in Topanga Canyon, where I can have a horse, and, well, you'll see ...

How come Topanga?

I've always wanted a horse, and I thought as long as I'm writing my own script and it's a new beginning, I might as well shoot for the moon. I still have the sailboat, though.

Well, that's good to know. I always thought you liked the boat.

Are you kidding? I loved the boat. When I'm on the water, my spirit blooms a million percent!

Okay, okay. I believe you.

You see, honey, Oleo said I would write a book about all that you and I did wrong and what we did right, and through the writing of it, I would help others to know that they weren't alone with their problems.

Yes, I remember.

Well, so far, it seems like all I've done is write about everything I did wrong when it came to you and me. Our story didn't have a happy ending. I want to use what I've learned from our mistakes to help someone, even if it's just through a fantasy that someone reading this can relate to.

All right, then tell us what happens next, Ms. Splendor, in your new life script.

I will, but honey, you have to remember that I will always love you no matter what.

And I you, Noelle, no matter what.

≈

4

A royal blue Mini Cooper with a white top and the license plate "MIGHTY" drove up Jonathan's Christmas lit street. Night had fallen. The puppy dog Kelly, wearing a pink ribbon on her collar, rode shotgun next to Noelle, who wore jeans, a T-shirt, and sneakers. When she reached Jonathan's house, she reached out to ring the security gate's bell.

Inga's voice could be heard over the security speakerphone. "May I help you?"

"Noelle Splendor to see Martin Weber."

Martin tried to read the newspaper, while Lucy obsessively paced up and down the library. Martin gave her annoyed glances, but she ignored him.

"Lucy, stop pacing!"

"I'm not pacing!"

"You are driving me crazy!"

"Where are Manny and Joey with Jonathan? Ms. Splendor is due any minute, and . . ."

"Lucy, Ms. Splendor will wait! Now, sit down!"

Lucy won't quit. "But I told Myrna to have dinner precisely at 7 p.m., and . . ."

Martin can't stand it. ". . . You are obsessing on everything!!"

"I don't know why you hired this . . . this person . . . Ms. Splendor. Surely, I can help Jonathan now that Melinda is out of the way. I mean . . . what I meant to say . . ."

Martin angrily threw his newspaper to the floor. "You ought to be ashamed of yourself!"

Lucy flipped her head innocently. "You're a fine one to be talking about shame, Father. How many murderers have you helped go free?"

"Shut up, Lucy!"

They were saved by a knock on the door.

Martin shouted gruffly, "Come in!"

Inga ushered in Noelle and Kelly. Martin stood to greet them, and Lucy's mouth dropped open. "A dog! Inga, get that animal out of here!"

As Inga moved to obey, Noelle stepped in front of Kelly to shield her. "We're all animals. Kelly is as smart as some people I meet."

Lucy flashed angrily, but Martin chuckled, shaking Noelle's hand.

"I'm Martin Weber . . . Noelle Splendor?"

"Yes. This is Kelly."

Kelly extended her paw. Martin laughed out loud, shaking with Kelly. "Hello, Kelly. You're a beautiful pup. What kind is she?"

Kelly wagged her tail happily and licked Martin's hand.

Noelle interpreted for her. "She says, 'Thanks,' and she's a lab terrier mix. Nine years old."

Martin nodded his acknowledgment to Kelly, and waved to Inga. "That'll be all, Inga."

Inga left.

Martin said to Noelle, "This is my daughter, Lucy Weber."

Noelle moved forward, her hand extended to shake. Kelly stayed right with her, and Lucy backed up, frightened, bumping into a chair.

Noelle said, "Kelly, sit."

Kelly did. Noelle put her flat hand in front of Kelly's face. "Stay."

Kelly obeyed. Noelle proceeded to a frozen Lucy, and shook her hand.

Lucy practically stuttered, "W-w-why . . . did you bring that . . . little . . . wolf?"

"Where I sleep, Kelly sleeps. She's very friendly. There's no need to be afraid of her." Kelly rolled over on her back and exposed her belly.

Martin laughed. Lucy gasped, "Ms. Splendor, you can't bring dog hair and drool into this home!"

Noelle returned to Kelly's side to say softly, "C'mon, Kelly," and they both walked toward the library door. "If you don't want Kelly, you don't want me. Goodnight, Martin."

Martin and Lucy exchanged surprised glances. Noelle opened the library door. Before she could exit, Martin called out to her.

"Wait! It's just that we weren't expecting..."

But before Martin could finish, Jonathan's yell was suddenly heard from the top of the staircase landing.

"Ow! Leave me alone, you stupid assed mother fuckers!"

Noelle, Kelly, and Martin ran into the foyer, and looked up the circular stairs, while Lucy watched from the library door.

Jonathan was shaved, and wearing a white dinner jacket, but his right arm was twisted up behind his back by Joey. Manny tried to grab Jonathan's flailing left arm.

"What is going on?!" Martin asked with exasperation.

Joey volunteered the information. "He took a couple more of those pain pills, and he's got vodka stashed everywhere!"

Jonathan struggled to get away from the two beefy men. "Let me go, you bastards! I can walk, goddamn it!"

"Let him go!" Martin said, annoyed.

Manny let go, but Joey held on. "He'll fall . . ."

"I said, let him go!" Martin roared.

Joey did. Jonathan took a step, and immediately tumbled down the wide carpeted stairs. Joey and Manny tried to catch him, but he reached the bottom, falling onto a thick Oriental rug.

Martin, Joey, and Manny ran to him. Lucy remained at the library door. Noelle noticed that Lucy didn't rush to help.

Martin called to Noelle. "Ms. Splendor, could you . . ."

The men moved away as Noelle approached. She expertly checked Jonathan for broken bones, while Kelly licked his face. Jonathan moaned, returning to consciousness.

He laughed at the surprise of Kelly. "Whoa! Where'd a dog come from?"

Jonathan tried to sit up. Noelle moved back, allowing him to do it on his own. He focused on her, and the smile on his face widened. "Who are you?"

"Noelle Splendor."

Jonathan rubbed his forehead. "Right. Ms. Splendor was coming."

"I'm here. This is Kelly."

"How ya doin', Kelly?" Jonathan scratched Kelly's ears, and tried to stand, but he fell back down.

Martin, Joey, and Manny jumped to help him, but Noelle stopped them. "No. Let him do it himself."

Jonathan managed to stand, leaning against the wall for support.

Martin looked around the foyer. "Where's your cane?"

Jonathan waved him away. "Don't need it for a sprained ankle!"

Joey cleared his throat. "He threw it out the window, sir."

Martin said, "Manny, go get it."

Noelle motioned for Manny to stop. "He said, he doesn't need it."

Martin smiled his understanding at her intervention. "All right, Ms. Splendor, you're on."

Noelle smiled. "Martin, call me, Noelle."

Jonathan struggled to stand. "Just who the hell are you?"

Before Noelle could answer him, Martin said, "Let's go into the library, and discuss this."

Noelle slapped her thigh for Kelly to come to her side. "And Kelly?"

Martin glanced over his shoulder at a stoic Lucy. "Kelly is welcome here."

Lucy turned her stiff back on all of them, and marched into the library.

Lucy went straight to the bar. She poured vodka into three glasses over ice, taking a solid swallow from one of them. She handed a drink to Jonathan, who acted surprise she was offering him one. Lucy gave the third drink to Martin, and turned to Noelle.

"Ms. Splendor, what will you have?"

"Club soda, please," Noelle said. "And, Lucy, call me, Noelle."

Lucy stiffened yet again. "The employees call me, Ms. Weber."

"I'm not an employee."

Lucy whipped around to Martin. "But, Father, didn't you hire Ms. Splendor . . . Noelle . . . for Jonathan?"

"Yes, but . . ."

Before Martin could finish, Jonathan's interest was piqued. "So that's why you're here?"

Noelle said, "Yes, but I'm an independent contractor."

Lucy laughed, while she found, then poured the club soda. "Oh, excuse me . . . I suppose prostitutes are self-employed, although I think pimps might take issue with that."

Martin was embarrassed. "Lucy, Noelle isn't a prostitute."

Lucy stopped laughing, but Jonathan chuckled. "The jeans and T-shirt told you that. What do you do, Noelle?"

"I'm a teacher," Noelle said calmly.

Lucy sniffed haughtily, "What do you teach?"

"I teach people how to adapt to their environment, when they find themselves acting crazy."

Jonathan rapidly downed his drink, and headed to the bar for another one. "What the hell does that mean?"

"Your father told me your drinking has made you dysfunctional."

Jonathan angrily glared at Martin. "Oh, he did, did he? What else did he tell you?"

Noelle plowed through. "You have a one month deadline."

Jonathan emptied a vodka bottle, and quickly opened another. "Hah! A *dead*line! And your plan?"

"Kelly and I will be with you 24 hours a day until the end of the month. Then we'll see you weekly."

"How much is my old man paying you?"

"$100 an hour."

Martin said seriously, "Maybe I'll have you pay her, son."

Jonathan did the math in his head. His eyes opened wide. "But 24 hours a day for 30 days is $72,000!"

"That's correct," Noelle replied.

Jonathan was no longer laughing, but Lucy was. She snorted, "There are no $1000 hookers, only $1000 johns!

Martin stood, pushing a button on a console next to the bar.

"Lucy, I don't need to justify my behavior to either one of you, and you could learn a few things from Ms. Splendor!"

Lucy scowled, and walked away. There was a knock on the door.

Martin called out, "Come in, Manny."

Manny entered, and bowed his head. "Someone rang for me, sir."

Martin nodded. "Yes, Manny, please show Ms. Splendor and Kelly to the room next to Billy's. Noelle, I apologize for my children's rudeness."

"I don't take it personally," Noelle said.

"Smart woman," Jonathan commented.

Martin smiled. "Never doubted it, Jonathan. Dinner is at seven, Noelle. We'll see you then."

Noelle, Kelly, and Manny exited. Martin turned around to Jonathan and Lucy. "You two, come with me."

Martin led Jonathan and Lucy into the small surveillance room off the library, where they all sat down. "What the hell have I raised?" he asked them in disgust.

Jonathan and Lucy looked away from him and each other. Martin turned on the TV monitors, and tuned in Billy in his bedroom playing Nintendo, and wearing a headset.

Martin flipped the TV monitor to a view of the kitchen, where Manny introduced Noelle and Kelly to Myrna, Inga, and Joey.

"I think Noelle Splendor is okay," Martin said.

"Yes, but you picked Melinda," Lucy replied.

Jonathan stood up precariously. "You bitch! I loved Melinda! What was wrong with her?"

Lucy pulled a 'Living Room' videotape out of a rack. "Maybe you need to be reminded how crazy you both acted, getting drunk on your daughter's birthday!"

Martin grabbed the tape from Lucy, and slapped it back onto the TV console. "That marriage was business."

Jonathan said sourly, "Ms. Splendor's arrangement is, too."

Lucy laughed. "I think Noelle the Good Witch is taking you for a ride, Father."

Jonathan said, "I think you're both crazy. I'm leaving to find a new environment. Let her teach you to adapt."

"But where will you go?" Martin asked.

"Anywhere but here!" Jonathan said.

Martin shook his head sadly. "Vito won't let you go."

Jonathan replied, "He'll have to find me first."

Lucy said, "All he'll have to do is follow the empty vodka bottles."

Jonathan leaned in to strangle Lucy. "I'm gonna kill you!"

Lucy struggled to get him off of her. Martin helped her, and they both finally pushed him away. Jonathan fell into a chair, suddenly sapped of strength. "I hate this life! Father, why did you sentence us to such misery?"

"I fell in love with your mother. Her family accepted me."

"But why did you have to work with Uncle Vito? Couldn't you have just been a regular brother-in-law?" Jonathan asked.

"I was young and hungry," Martin said. "It didn't make sense to say no. By the time I knew the family's business, I was in too deeply to get out."

On the surveillance monitor, they watched Manny bring Noelle and Kelly into their bedroom.

Jonathan shook his head sadly. "And now you've brought in Noelle Splendor."

Lucy asked, "What did you tell her, Father?"

"That we're criminal attorneys. Jonathan lost his wife and daughter in a car accident, and he's got a drinking problem."

They observed Kelly sniffing the room, while Noelle unpacked. Jonathan leaned in closer, watching them.

"Get out while you can, Noelle!"

≈

5

Christmas lights in the backyard could be seen from Noelle's window, and Kelly had her fore-paws up on the windowsill, taking in the view.

The bedroom door was ajar, and Billy stuck his head in snottily. "Who are you?"

"Noelle Splendor. Who are you?"

"Billy Weber. Who's that?"

Billy entered, pointing to Kelly, who approached him with her tail wagging.

Noelle introduced them. "Kelly, this is Billy."

Kelly extended her paw. Billy took it, and admired the pup. "Bitchin'!"

"She is a female," Noelle said dryly.

Billy realized Noelle was unpacking. He got excited. "Are you staying here?"

"Yes, for a while."

"Is Kelly?

"Yes."

"Aunt Lucy's gonna be pissed!"

Noelle smiled and nodded. "I think that's an accurate assessment, and . . ." Noelle checked her watch. "It's time for dinner."

~

Martin and Lucy argued in the dining room.

Martin was very annoyed. "Lucy, for a smart woman, you do some stupid things! Inga, hurry up!"

Inga rushed in, carrying a place setting. Manny accompanied her.

Lucy answered defensively. "How was I to know you wouldn't want her to eat in the kitchen with the rest of the help?"

Manny moved the other place settings over to make room for the extra one, as Noelle, Billy, and Kelly entered.

Lucy edged away from Kelly. "No! That dog won't eat in here with us!"

Noelle remained calm. "Where I eat, Kelly eats."

"She'll drool," Lucy whined.

"Kelly doesn't drool," Noelle answered.

Jonathan limped in, carrying a glass of ice and the vodka bottle. "Does Kelly go to restaurants?" he asked.

"If they have an outside patio," Noelle responded.

Billy took his seat. "And if they don't?"

Noelle said solemnly. "I find one that does."

Jonathan whistled. "Someone with personal integrity!" He plopped down at the head of the table.

Martin motioned Noelle to sit. Manny placed a dish of dog food in a corner of the dining room.

"I've been known to falter," Noelle said.

"It's good to know you're human . . ." Lucy smiled nastily.

Martin threw Lucy a withering look as they took their seats.

Manny stood at attention. "Which wine tonight, sir?"

Jonathan laughed, turning to Noelle. "I'm allowed to drink?"

Noelle nodded. "I'm observing you in your natural habitat on New Year's Eve. We start tomorrow."

Jonathan snickered. "What's this we, kimo sabe? Manny, surprise me!"

Manny bowed his head, and exited.

Noelle commented, "My students often resist change."

"How do you deal with that?" Lucy asked.

"I'm in charge of their environment," Noelle answered.

Jonathan laughed, pouring himself more vodka. "Hah! Lucy's been staying with us since my wife died."

Noelle looked pointedly at Lucy. "Lucy may prefer to return home."

Lucy's eyes registered the insult, and Jonathan laughed again. Martin felt compelled to speak. "Noelle, tact isn't one of your strong points."

Noelle shrugged her shoulders. "I don't pretend to be a politician or a lawyer."

Jonathan stomped his fist down on the dining room table. "Well, you're in a room full of lawyers! Aren't we all the picture of decorum?"

Jonathan downed his vodka, flipped the last ice cube in his glass up into the air, and caught it in his mouth on its way down. "Tah-dah! Happy New Year!"

Everyone stared at him blankly. Billy was the first to speak. "Don't you ever embarrass yourself, Dad?"

Jonathan snapped at him. "Just never you mind!"

≈

Noelle and Kelly exited the house through the pool patio door. They walked to the lawn surrounded by Christmas lights. Noelle extended her arms, and turned around in a circle.

"Free time, Kelly!"

Kelly joyfully jumped into the air, tail wagging. Noelle threw a tennis ball, and Kelly ran after it with abandon. Noelle could see fireworks in the distant sky.

"Happy New Year, Kelly!"

Kelly scooped up the tennis ball in her mouth, and raced back to Noelle, who knelt to hug her tightly.

Billy wistfully watched their affectionate play from his bedroom window.

≈

Jonathan was passed out on his own bed, arm extended to the floor. His hand held an empty vodka bottle. The television blared "Auld Lang Syne" from New York's Times Square.

≈

Lucy sat in the television light of the library, watching the same Times Square scene, but the sound was muted. She pulled out her cocaine vial, and took several hits. Then she picked up the telephone and dialed.

"Vito, it's Lucy . . . My father hired a bimbo to dry out Jonathan, and they want me gone . . . Okay, I'll check back in the morning before I fly to New York."

Lucy hung up, and dialed another number. "Louie, I'm on way to your place."

≈

New Year's Day had a pink sunrise, and Noelle and Kelly witnessed it, as they walked around the lawn in Jonathan's backyard.

Noelle checked her watch, and she led Kelly into the house, up the circular stairs. They padded quietly toward Jonathan's bedroom. Noelle knocked softly. She put her ear to the door to listen for a response. Nothing.

Noelle whispered to Kelly. "I don't think Jonathan's up yet, Kelly. What do you think?"

Kelly wagged her tail, and nudged the doorknob with her nose. Noelle laughed. "Okay, good idea."

Noelle and Kelly entered Jonathan's bedroom. Jonathan was on the floor next to the bed in the fetal position.

Noelle knelt near him, and Kelly gently licked Jonathan's face. Jonathan was startled awake. "I didn't do anything wrong!"

"It's okay," Noelle said. "You're okay, Jonathan."

Jonathan rubbed his eyes and his head. "What time is it?"

"Dawn."

"What's wrong?"

"Nothing. Time to wake up. Early bird gets the worm."

"What?!"

"Kelly and I are ready to work."

"Well, good for you! I'm goin' back to sleep." Jonathan curled back into a sleeping position.

Noelle said, "Kelly, kiss Jonathan."

Kelly licked Jonathan's face happily. Jonathan pushed her away. "Stop it!" He lightly tapped Kelly on the nose.

Noelle grabbed Jonathan's wrist. "Hey, don't hit Kelly!"

"People are always hitting dogs!" Jonathan said defensively.

Noelle's eyes squinted. "Well, don't hit one when I'm around! Now, it's time to get started!"

Jonathan grumbled, "Who made you King Shit!"

"I'm here to work," Noelle said, "and you've run out of second chances."

"You don't know the half of it," Jonathan said sadly.

"What do you mean?" Noelle asked.

Jonathan considered Noelle's compassionate face. He sat up. "Never mind. How do we start?"

Noelle smiled. "Wake up Billy."

"Why Billy?"

"He lives with you."

"Yeah, well, people have a way of disappearing around here," Jonathan said, looking away into the distance.

Noelle spoke quietly. "Your wife and daughter?"

Pain crossed Jonathan's face. He awkwardly stood, and walked to his dresser. He handed Noelle a framed family photograph.

"Jenny's fifth birthday. Six months ago. Blowin' out the candles with Melinda."

Noelle studied the picture. "They were both very beautiful."

"Yeah." Jonathan stared at the floor. He didn't want to be sad. He grabbed the photograph back, put it in a drawer, and took out a pair of sweat pants.

"You gonna watch me dress?"

Noelle turned around, so her back faced him. Jonathan removed his PJs, and Kelly sniffed his butt.

"Hey, stop that, Kelly!"

"What's she doing now?" Noelle asked, straining to turn only part of the way.

"Smelling my butt!" Jonathan jumped around, trying to avoid Kelly's inquisitive nose.

Noelle laughed. "She's not afraid of dark places. You know, you don't have to hide that picture. It's healthy to cry during mourning."

"Maybe health doesn't interest me."

"What does interest you?"

"Escape. You gonna watch me pee?" Jonathan headed to the bathroom.

"No, but leave the door open," Noelle said. "I don't want any stashed vodka making an appearance."

"Aw, Teach, don't you trust me?"

"Only to take care of yourself."

~

6

Billy was asleep on his bed in his jeans, T-shirt, and sneakers, and still wearing his headphones. Jonathan, Noelle, and Kelly entered.

Jonathan gently took off the headphones. "He likes to block out reality."

"Denial runs in the family. Kelly, kiss Billy."

Kelly licked Billy awake. "Hey! What?! Hi, Kelly!" Billy hugged the dog.

"Wanna go for a walk with us, Billy?" Noelle asked.

"Okay! Let's go!" Billy jumped out of bed, playing with Kelly.

"Sure, for fun he's up at the crack of dawn!" Jonathan complained. "For school, it's always 'Five more minutes. Five more!'"

"Aw, Dad . . ."

"Don't 'Aw, Dad' me, and leave the head-phones here."

"No! I don't want to!"

"It's all right," Noelle said. "He can bring them."

Jonathan saluted Noelle, then bowed, making a grand gesture. "No mutiny here, Captain Splendor!"

Noelle laughed, and they all traipsed out of the room.

As they entered the backyard, Billy and Kelly ran ahead of Jonathan and Noelle. Noelle threw a tennis ball, and Kelly caught it in her mouth. "Kelly, let's play Keep Away!"

Kelly dropped the ball in front of Noelle. As soon as Noelle grabbed for it, Kelly whisked the ball away, then dropped it again. When Noelle tried to pick it up, Kelly scooped up the prize.

Noelle called out, "Billy, try to get it before Kelly."

But Kelly was faster every time. Billy squealed with delight, chasing Kelly across the yard. Jonathan watched, enjoying the scene vicariously.

Noelle ran up to him. "Your turn, Jonathan."

"Billy deserves some fun."

"He'll have fun watching you."

"But I have a sprained ankle."

"Kelly won't mind."

"But . . ."

"How many excuses do you have?"

Jonathan cocked his head to one side, smiling at Noelle. "Kelly, bring me the ball."

Kelly dropped it at Jonathan's feet. As soon as Jonathan leaned down to pick it up, Kelly scooped up the ball, and dropped it a few feet away. Kelly rolled over on her back, proudly wagging her tail. Billy laughed.

Casually whistling, Jonathan quickly bent over, but before he could grab the ball, Kelly swept in, winning the treat. Billy and Noelle laughed together.

Jonathan had broken a sweat, and his mouth was parched. "Okay, Kelly wins. Orange juice time."

Noelle objected. "No way, Jose. You've only been working for two minutes."

"I'm thirsty."

"I bet. It's not time for a break."

"For me, it is!" Jonathan quickly limped out of the yard into the house.

"Billy, will you be in charge of Kelly, while I check on your Dad?"

"Wow! Can I really?"

"Kelly, stay here. Take care of Billy, and have fun!"

≈

Noelle ran into the house, and saw Jonathan turn a corner into the foyer.

Jonathan walked purposefully through the foyer toward the library. A man with a mission. Noelle stayed behind him.

Jonathan quickly walked across the library to the bar, where he found all the liquor gone. He slammed his fist down. "Son of a bitch! Fucking whore! Manny, where are you?!"

Jonathan furiously punched the console at the bar. His hands shook. He was sweating profusely. Noelle spoke to him from the doorway.

"Manny can't help you."

Jonathan whipped around, his eyes mad as a hatter. "Where's the liquor?"

"Inaccessible."

"You're all bitches and whores!"

Manny entered. "You rang, sir?"

"Bring me a fifth of vodka, Manny! Now!!"

"My orders are no alcohol, sir."

"Who the hell ordered you?"

"Ms. Splendor. Your father said I am to follow her orders."

Jonathan was apoplectic. "Who the hell is paying you?"

Manny remained composed. "Your father pays my salary, sir."

Jonathan registered a light bulb going off in his head. "And my sister hired you! I'm being set up like a stuck pig! I'm getting the fuck out of here!"

Jonathan ran out of the library. Following him, Noelle called out over her shoulder. "Manny, please ask Joey to bring up the family car with the map I gave him, and Billy and Kelly in the back seat."

Noelle disappeared through the door. Manny shook his head and sighed. "Rich people."

~

Jonathan limped into his bedroom, and started frantically emptying drawers all over the floor.

Noelle entered a moment later. He turned to her with venom in his eyes.

"You are a dangerous woman!"

"When you're drunk and unconscious, you're open to danger. I could have been a thief!"

"You are a thief! You've stolen my vodka, cash, ID, and checks!"

"And your credit cards."

"I'll go to the bank!"

"And your car keys."

Jonathan grabbed his pants from the chair, pulling the pockets inside out. Empty. He threw them at Noelle, who ducked.

"I'll walk!"

Jonathan stomped out of the room. Noelle followed him, smiling to herself.

Jonathan limped down the circular stairs with Noelle beside him. "Stop following me! You're fired!!"

Noelle stayed right with him. "You didn't hire me! Let me take you away from here."

"What's that mean? You have a place reserved six feet under?"

"You're the one killing yourself."

Jonathan ignored her, stalking out the front door.

He climbed into the bushes next to the front door. Noelle watched him bend down, and crawl out of sight. She crept after him.

"Jonathan, what are you doing? ... Jonathan? Where are you?"

Noelle turned a corner and found him drinking vodka directly from a pint bottle. He tried to cover two other bottles half-buried in the soil.

Noelle sat down with him in the dirt. "Let me take you to a place, where you can start fresh."

"No such place." Jonathan was already tipsy. His defenses were down.

"My house," Noelle suggested.

"Where's that?"

"Let me surprise you. Allow yourself to be blindfolded."

"You're kidnapping me?"

Noelle laughed. She stood, extending her hand. "An adventure between two consenting adults."

Jonathan took her hand, and stood shakily. They exited the shrubbery to find Joey pulling up in the Silver Rolls Royce with Billy and Kelly in back.

Jonathan was disappointed. "They're all coming, too?"

"Joey's just gonna drop us off. Here, put on this blindfold." Noelle pulled out a white hand-kerchief.

Jonathan balked. "Are you gonna whack me?"

"What do you mean?" Noelle asked.

"Kill me," Jonathan said.

"Nobody's trying to kill you," Noelle said reassuringly.

"How do you know!?" Jonathan demanded. "I'm a criminal attorney. People hate me!"

"I'm not trying to kill you!"

"But how do I know?!"

"Trust me." Noelle held out the blindfold. Jonathan stared at her intently, then turned for her to tie it over his eyes.

Billy leaned out of the car. "Cool, Dad. Where we goin'?"

Jonathan said, "Ask the Maestro," and let Noelle guide him into the front seat.

Noelle said, "Drive, Joey!" and she hopped in back.

As they pulled out of the gate, they didn't notice the limo with New York plates, coming up the street.

Lucy sat in back with Louie next to her. "Dominic, stop the car," she said. The chauffeur stopped, and Lucy hopped out. She leaned inside. "Follow them. I'll miss my plane to New York if I go with you."

Louie whined, "But can't Dominic do it alone? I was gonna take you to the airport."

Lucy barked, "Don't ask questions, Louie! Dominic, drive!"

Lucy slammed the door, and Dominic pulled away. She repeatedly rang the gate's bell until a harried Manny answered through the speakerphone, "Yes, Ms. Weber."

"Open the fucking gate!" Lucy snarled.

Lucy stormed up to the house. Just as she was about to ring the bell, Manny opened the front door. Lucy brushed past him to go inside. She walked to the telephone table, and picked up a cell phone.

Slapping it hard into her hand, Lucy snapped at Manny. "Where'd Jonathan go?"

"Ms. Splendor gave Joey a map," Manny said, "but I didn't see it."

Lucy couldn't believe it. "You let them go without knowing where?!"

Manny's back stiffened. "It is not my job to question Mr. Weber's itinerary."

Lucy practically bared her teeth in anger. "Don't smart mouth me, Manny. I know how much hard time you've done for forgery!"

Manny flinched. Lucy paced, slapping the phone even harder into her hand. "What else has happened since I left?"

"Ms. Splendor had us remove all alcohol and pills."

"Did she find any hidden?"

"Quite a bit."

"What else?"

"She confiscated Mr. Weber's money, ID, and keys."

Lucy stopped in her tracks. "What the hell did she do with them?!"

Manny almost smiled. "Ms. Splendor did not reveal that information to me."

"I bet!" Lucy walked to the library. "Manny, there's a packed suitcase in my room. Put it into Jonathan's other car, and get ready to drive me to the airport. Have Inga bring me some coffee with brandy in it."

"But, Ms. Weber," Manny protested, "I told you, there is no more alcohol in the house."

Lucy was exasperated. "What did she do with all of it?"

Manny was enjoying her frustration. "We poured it out."

Lucy frowned. "This bitch isn't fooling around . . ."

7

Lucy slammed the library door behind her, and dropped the phone on a chair. She nervously got out her cocaine, and took a hit. Then she carefully put some on her finger, and massaged it onto her teeth and gums.

Lucy picked up the phone, and dialed, looking through empty bar cabinets while she waited for the other party to answer. She anxiously tapped her long fingernails against the wood of the cabinets.

"Yes, hi, Vito, it's Lucy. Jonathan's disappearing. I've got Louie following him . . ."

The sun sparkled on the Pacific Ocean next to the Pacific Coast Highway. The limousine trailed the Rolls Royce by several cars.

Inside the Rolls, Billy and Kelly shared a back seat window, putting their faces into the wind. Noelle smiled at their enjoyment.

In front, Jonathan still wore the blindfold, but turned his face toward Noelle. "Why the blindfold, Noelle?"

"I don't want you to know which direction your house is," she responded.

"But how come?" he persisted.

Noelle smiled. "Too many temptations."

Jonathan lifted his nose to the open window. "But I can smell the ocean, so I know we came west . . ."

≈

Louie's cell phone rang in the limo. He answered. "Yeah . . . okay."

Louie disconnected the line. He seemed puzzled, and sighed. "Dominic," he said sadly, "We're gonna take 'em out."

Dominic tightened his grip on the steering wheel, and pressed down on the gas. He changed lanes, and sped up to catch the Rolls Royce.

~

Billy leaned over the front seat to reach the radio, and in doing so, jostled the blindfolded Jonathan. "Hey, what's going on?"

"I want the radio on," Billy said matter-of-factly.

"So ask Joey," Jonathan answered crossly. "Now, sit down."

Billy sat back in his seat, sulking. When he didn't say anything, Jonathan got more annoyed. "Well, Joey . . . put on the radio!"

Joey reached out to turn it on, but Noelle interceded. "No, Joey. Billy hasn't asked you."

Jonathan laughed. "You seemed awfully easy on the kid earlier."

Noelle touched Billy's arm kindly. "When people ask for what they want, most of the time they get it. Asking is half the battle."

Billy smiled at her shyly, and said clearly, "Joey, will you please turn on the radio?"

Joey checked the rear view mirror for Noelle's okay, and he also noticed the limo with

New York plates rapidly gaining on them. "Uh oh, trouble."

"What's wrong?" Noelle asked.

Jonathan ripped off his blindfold, and saw the limo right behind them. "The limo with New York plates!"

Joey pressed his foot down harder on the accelerator. Jonathan watched his hands tighten on the steering wheel. "Who are they, Joey?"

Joey's scared eyes kept checking the rear view mirror. "I don't know who's drivin', but the car belongs to the family."

Suddenly, the limo changed lanes, pulling up alongside Joey. The limo's passenger window opened. It was Louie, aiming his gun.

Jonathan was shocked. "Louie!!"

Joey jammed his foot down on the accelerator, pulling away into traffic. The limo followed right behind. Joey pulled out his .357 Magnum.

Noelle did a double take. "Joey's got a gun, too?! Who are you guys?"

"That was Cousin Louie!" Billy yelled.

Jonathan bellowed, "Joey, get us out of here! Billy, Noelle, get down on the floor!"

Billy dove down, but Noelle kept her head up, scanning every direction. "What the hell's going on?"

Joey was driving erratically, constantly checking his rear view mirror. "Louie told me, Vito always says to watch his back!"

Joey's tires screamed as he veered across lanes and the terrifying curves of Pacific Coast Highway. Noelle wouldn't kneel down. "Who's Vito?"

Jonathan said tensely, "Somebody who wants me dead!" He pushed Noelle's head between the seats. "Now get down, and stay down, goddamn it!"

The limo caught up to them again. Louie tried to aim his gun between the speeding vehicles, and suddenly, Noelle spied their escape route.

"Joey, get off the highway. Turn into Topanga Canyon now!"

Joey cut across traffic, causing other cars to crash behind him. The limo careened past the wreckage, pursuing the Rolls Royce into the Santa Monica mountains.

Noelle saw a filling station. "Joey, turn at the gas station!"

Joey cruised the corner at a very fast clip. He hit a metal display sign, which glanced off the car, and sliced the gas pump in half. An explosion ripped into the air. People scattered to get out of the way.

Billy yelled, "All right!!"

The Rolls raced past the fire. The limo kept up behind them through the winding mountain roads. Sirens could be heard in the distance.

Joey turned too wide, taking out a stop sign. Suddenly, the limo was right there. Louie aimed and fired. Joey ducked. Jonathan jumped, but the bullet hit his shoulder. "I'm hit!"

Louie fired again, nailing Joey in the head. Joey slumped over, dead at the wheel, blood all over his blown-up face.

The Rolls Royce ran right into a muddy ditch. The car leaned at an angle, its front tires in the mud. The limo kept going.

～

Joey's dead body had fallen on top of an unconscious Jonathan, whose head rested against the dashboard. Blood was everywhere.

In the back seat, Kelly licked Noelle, whose eyes darted open. She sat up, rubbing her head. Billy moaned, trying to get up.

Noelle gently touched his face. "Billy, are you okay?"

Billy nodded. "Yeah . . . I think so."

Noelle flexed her neck. "Jonathan, are you?"

No answer. Noelle and Billy's eyes met for one terrified instant, and then they leaned over the front seat, where they saw the injured men. They jumped out of the car with Kelly scooting out behind them.

Noelle opened the passenger door, and carefully pushed Joey off Jonathan. She knelt down, checking Jonathan's pulse. "Jonathan, can you hear me?!"

Kelly licked Jonathan's face. Billy stood right next to Noelle. "Is my Dad dead?"

"No, but his pulse is pretty weak." Noelle searched for Jonathan's wound. She used his blindfold as a pressure bandage, then put Billy's hand on top of it. "Push down on the wound to stop the bleeding."

Billy did it, and watched while Noelle checked Joey's pulse. "What about Joey?"

"Dead," Noelle said soberly. "But, Billy, I think we can save your Dad."

Billy nodded with frightened eyes. Noelle took over on the pressure bandage, and put her other hand on Billy's shoulder. "While I keep him from bleeding, I want you to run to the gas station that exploded. Bring back an ambulance and the police."

"No!" Billy cried. "I'll get lost!"

Noelle smiled reassuringly. "Take Kelly with you. She'll find me on the way back. To get to the gas station, just look in the sky, and follow the smoke from the fire at the gas pump."

Noelle pointed to the sky. Billy looked up, and saw the direction the smoke was coming from. Just as he nodded his okay, Jonathan moaned.

Noelle touched his forehead. "Jonathan, Billy's going for help."

"No!" Jonathan coughed, and whispered, "No . . . cops!"

Noelle was astounded. "What?! Why not?"

Drifting in and out of consciousness, Jonathan spoke slowly. "No cops . . . family business . . ."

"But you could die!" Noelle pleaded. "You've got a bullet in your shoulder!"

"You . . . take it out . . ." Jonathan murmured.

Noelle recoiled. "I never took a bullet out!"

"Easy . . . I'll walk you . . . through it."

Noelle backed up, shaking her head. "No way! You need to see a doctor!"

"They . . . call cops . . . on bullets."

"Doesn't your family have a doctor?"

"He'll . . . tell . . . Vito!"

"Who the hell is this Vito?"

Billy answered that one. "Uncle Vito is my grandpa's brother-in-law."

Jonathan forced out, "He's . . . trying . . . to kill me."

"But, Jonathan . . ."

"Please, Noelle . . . You've got to . . . believe me . . . I can't go home again! You were . . . takin' me to your house . . . Does my father know . . . where you live?"

"No, but . . ."

". . . We can hide there . . ."

". . . But . . ."

Jonathan moaned, losing consciousness. Noelle became resolute.

"Billy, I'm gonna need your help."

Billy was terrified, holding back tears. Noelle firmly took his hand, and put it back on top of Jonathan's pressure bandage.

"Keep pushing down hard to stop the bleeding." Noelle turned to Kelly. "Kelly, stay with Billy and Jonathan."

Billy watched Noelle open the driver's door. She heaved Joey out of the car, and pushed him into the ditch. Noelle saw Joey's gun near the gas pedal. She put it in the trunk as well, then went back to the task at hand, which was to get the hell out of there.

Noelle substituted her hand for Billy's on Jonathan's bandage, as she climbed back into the Rolls Royce. She started issuing directions.

"Kelly, get in the car. Billy, close the doors, and climb into the front seat to hold this bandage."

Kelly jumped in. Billy slammed both doors, and scrambled over to Jonathan, who moaned with the vibrations of the car movements.

Noelle slowed Billy down. "Be careful, honey."

Billy got settled, holding the pressure bandage. Noelle started the motor.

Jonathan moaned again, opening his eyes. "What's goin' on?"

Noelle smiled grimly. "We're gettin' the hell outta here!"

Noelle put the car into reverse, and stepped on the gas, but the front tires spun in the muddy ditch. She sighed, frustrated. "Have you ever driven a car, Billy?"

"Grandpa Martin let me once in a big field."

Jonathan mumbled, "Sons a bitches . . . never told me."

"You were drunk when we told you!" Billy retorted.

"Little brat . . . I oughta . . ."

Noelle interrupted his tirade. "Jonathan, this little brat has been helping keep you alive!"

Jonathan saw Billy's hand pushing as hard as he could on his father's bloody shoulder. Jonathan put his own hand on top of Billy's. "Thanks, pal."

They smiled at each other.

Noelle clapped her hands. "Okay! Jonathan, keep pressure on your wound. I'm gonna push, and Billy's gonna guide us out of the mud real slow."

Noelle slipped and slid into the ditch in front of the car. "Billy, put her in reverse."

Billy could barely see over the wheel, and his feet could hardly reach the pedals.

Jonathan enjoyed watching Billy stretch. "It's okay, son. We'll do it together. Sit up close, and I'll work the gas and brake."

Jonathan slid his leg to the accelerator. All three did their bit, and the Rolls was backed out of the ditch.

Noelle hopped back into the car, patting Jonathan and Billy on their backs. "Thanks, guys, you were great!"

They both smiled proudly.

Noelle pulled the car onto the road. As she went over the bumps, Jonathan moaned, but then began to sing a Willie Nelson song: "On the road again, I can't wait to get on the road again . . ."

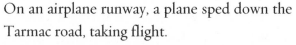

8

On an airplane runway, a plane sped down the Tarmac road, taking flight.

Lucy was the only passenger on this private jet. Her nails dug into her seat as the plane went to a higher altitude before leveling off. She relaxed her grip to take out her cocaine.

Lucy did up a spoonful, then pushed a button, and picked up a cell phone. As she punched in the numbers, a stewardess appeared.

"Did you ring, Ms. Weber?"

"More coffee with brandy!" Lucy waved the stewardess away, then spoke conspiratorially into the telephone.

"Louie, report . . ." Lucy listened for a moment, then suddenly burst into anger. "You idiot! You don't know if Jonathan's dead! You fucked up Christmas Day, and now you fucked up again!"

～～

The limo was parked, overlooking the Santa Monica mountains. Dominic sat behind the wheel, taking a nap. Louie leaned on the hood of the limo, drinking a bottle of beer, and talking to Lucy.

"I'm tellin' ya, baby, he's probably dead. I know I hit him, but there were sirens everywhere, cuz of that gasoline explosion Joey triggered. We had to get outta there. We've been waitin' for you to call like you said."

Lucy looked over her shoulder nervously. "You didn't tell Vito, did you?"

"Nah. Why would I do that?" Louie asked. "You told me to wait for your call."

"Just checking. Remember, we're supposed to take care of this one. We don't bother Vito. Got it?"

"Got it."

"Go back to the ditch and check. I'll call you again. This time, make sure Jonathan's dead!"

≈

Topanga Canyon glistened in the sunlight, as Noelle drove through the mountains until she reached a wooden mailbox. She turned, going down a bumpy hill into a flat clearing.

Noelle parked next to a wooden cabin. Behind the cabin was a stable and corral.

Billy noticed a healthy horse eating alfalfa. "Look, Dad, a horse!"

Noelle smiled. "That's Missy the Mare."

Jonathan nodded, but his eyelids were getting heavy. "Nice . . . but I don't feel so good."

Noelle realized that in his wooziness, Jonathan had stopped applying pressure to his wound, and his blood was oozing out. "Quick! Let's get him inside!"

The one room cabin was spacious. Noelle and Billy dragged Jonathan onto a king-sized bed set up in a corner. Noelle felt his head.

"He's developing a fever! Billy, apply pressure to his shoulder!"

Billy used the bloody handkerchief. Noelle disappeared into a bathroom, and his eyes wandered. He saw paintings with Noelle's signature, a big bay window overlooking Missy the Mare's corral, a large globe, a sailboat in a bottle, a TV, VCR/DVD player, and stereo.

Then Noelle was back. She carried a hemostat, a jar of Sulfa powder, smelling salts, bandages, and a wet cloth. She put the smelling salts under Jonathan's nose. He came to, pushing the irritant away.

Noelle cleaned the wound with the wet cloth. "Jonathan, I'm going to try and take the bullet out now. I have a hemostat to lift it out."

". . . Pain killers . . ."

"None, but I've got Sulfa powder to beat the infection."

". . . Just . . . stick in the hemostat . . ."

Billy swallowed nervously. "Doesn't she have to cut you open?"

Jonathan chuckled softly. ". . . Hope not . . . Gimme somethin' to bite down on . . . for the pain . . ."

"Will this leather belt work?" Noelle removed her belt. Jonathan bit down on the leather.

Noelle breathed deeply, and stuck in the hemostat. Jonathan jumped, his face contorted in pain. Billy tried not to cry, and hugged Kelly for support.

Noelle pulled the bullet out, dropping it onto the night table. She poured the Sulfa powder onto the open wound, and put on a clean bandage.

Jonathan started drifting into sleep. "I need . . . a nap . . ."

Noelle laughed, walking to open the top half of a Dutch door, which led to her backyard. She took a deep breath of fresh air.

"What a morning . . . Happy New Year!"

≈

Well, honey . . .

I like him.

I do, too. I think I can love him because he's one of the fraternity.

And what fraternity is that?

He's one of the good guys.

His white hat is a little gray, Noelle.

That's okay. So was yours. Nobody's perfect.

I recognize myself in him.

Yes, well, we write from what we know, and I knew you awfully well. You don't mind, do you?

No. It's for a good cause . . . your happiness . . . and that means a lot to me. More than you know.

I want to believe that.

Then believe it, and it's true.

That gives me goose bumps.

The truth will do that.

Honey, what's it like there for you? What will happen to you now?

The most comprehensive thing I can tell you is that heaven is indeed heavenly, thus its name, and what will happen to me is as much a mystery here, as it was on earth. The unknown remains unknowable. You may remember an old friend of ours once said that "there" is no better than "here." When your "there" has become "here," you will simply obtain another "there" that will, again, look better than "here."

Yes, I will always remember that. He's a very wise man.

I think it's best if we focus on your story. Let's unfold your thoughts and see if you can write yourself a happy ending.

All right.

Now where were we?

It had been a helluva New Year's morning...

9

Dominic parked the limo near the ditch, where they'd left the Rolls Royce. He and Louie got out. Dominic checked over his shoulder, as they approached Joey's dead body.

Louie noticed the departing tire tracks. "Uh-oh. Where's Jonathan?"

Dominic got very nervous, and started dancing on his toes. "We better get outta here, before they pin Joey's murder on us!"

Louie tried to calm him. "It's okay, Dom. The cops don't know about it yet, or they woulda taken Joey's body, and cordoned off the area."

Louie quickly walked through the mud to Joey's body. "Yeech! I hate mud!"

Dominic kept checking over his shoulder. "Anybody could see us, Louie!"

"I gotta make sure he's dead!"

"He's dead, man, I'm tellin' ya!"

Louie got annoyed. "Dominic, go get in the car!"

Dominic was only too happy to oblige. He ran like a scared rabbit back to the limo.

Louie checked Joey's pulse. "Dead . . . shit . . . I'll miss ya, Joey the Clown. It was nothin' personal. Just business."

~~

Kelly led the way for Noelle and Billy to enter the corral in Noelle's backyard. Missy the Mare whinnied at the visitors. Noelle held out her hand to the horse.

"C'mere, Missy. This is Billy."

The horse approached them, and Noelle petted the mare's sleek face. Billy excitedly stood on his tippy toes to touch Missy.

Noelle furrowed her brow in thought. "Billy, did you say the man in the limousine was your cousin?"

"Yeah. Cousin Louie. Do you think he was playing a game, like pretending to be a Ninja?"

"Some game. Your Dad seems sure your Uncle Vito is behind this."

"Uncle Vito likes games. Can I take a ride on Missy?"

Noelle ruffled Billy's hair. "I know you can ... You're able to. The question is, may you."

"May I ride Missy?" Billy asked promptly.

Noelle answered by opening the corral, lifting Billy onto the horse's bare back, and guiding them into a big circle.

Billy was very excited. "I wish my Mom could see me!"

Noelle walked alongside, holding Missy's tether. "Billy, aren't you still scared?"

Billy shrugged his shoulders. "When my Mom and Jenny died, Grandpa Martin told me everybody dies. He said, practice dying. Live everyday like it's our last, and we'll be happy."

Noelle chuckled. "Smart man. He knows philosophy."

"Phil who?" Billy asked.

"Philosophy," laughed Noelle. "The love of thinking.

"Oh," Billy said. "I like it here, Noelle. I'll be back tomorrow."

Noelle was touched, but before she could reply, Billy spontaneously bent over to hug her. She hugged him back, and cradled his head.

≈

The ocean sparkled next to a patio, where Louie ate in a Malibu restaurant. Empty beer bottles and another meal were on the table.

Just as Louie was about to take a bite of his food, his cell phone rang. Louie sighed, and answered it.

"Yeah . . ."

On the airplane, Lucy had her shoes off, feet up, and her long black hair was down around her shoulders. A 3/4 empty wine bottle sat next to her cocaine vial and unfinished lunch.

Lucy poured a full glass of wine, while she slurred to Louie. "What are you doin'?"

"Eatin' lunch." Louie began to eat while he listened.

"Me, too. I'm almost to New York." Lucy drank some more wine. "I had fun in your bed last night, Big Louie."

Louie drank some more beer. "Me, too. I miss ya, baby."

"I told ya, it's a couple of days. I'm taking care of this murdering Santa Claus cousin, since Jonathan didn't want the job."

Louie took a big bite of burger. Lucy took a big slurp of wine. She dipped her finger in the wine, then sensually sucked her finger.

"Hey, Big Louie . . ."

Dominic joined him at the table, and Louie answered her with a mouthful. "Yeah . . ."

"How 'bout I pretend to suck that big cock of yours, and talk you off like one of those 976 babes?"

Louie almost choked on his food by swallowing the mouthful whole.

Dominic alerted to the trouble. "You okay, Big Louie?"

Louie swigged a beer. "Yeah . . . I'm fine."

He spoke formally into the phone. "Listen, I'm in a restaurant in Malibu. Dominic just came in, so maybe I could do this later?"

Lucy laughed. "Okay, how 'bout Jonathan and pals?"

Louie cleared his throat. "Joey's dead. The Rolls is gone. We followed the muddy tire tracks for a while into Topanga Canyon, but the mud got less and less, so we haven't found anything." Louie took another bite, chewing over the phone's mouthpiece.

Lucy slammed her feet down off the seat in front of her. "So you're tellin' me Jonathan's still alive, and you're eatin' lunch instead of lookin' for him!"

Louie stopped mid-chew. He talked with food in his mouth. "I gotta eat . . ."

Lucy stood, knocking over her lunch tray. "Spit out that fucking food!"

Louie spit the food into his plate. Dominic stopped eating, his eyes wide. Louie was embarrassed.

Lucy paced on the plane. "Change cars. Comb every inch of Topanga, and tell Manny to call if they come home. That woman must be hiding them, and I want to know where the fuck they are!"

10

Billy and Kelly ran ahead of Noelle in the backyard toward the cabin. Noelle called out to them.

"Kelly, stop in the herb garden, so we can make some lunch."

Kelly guided Billy to an herb garden, sniffing everything on the way. Noelle bent down, picking off pieces of plants. Billy watched her intently.

"Will you help me, Billy?"

"What do I do?"

Noelle pointed. "Pinch some mint for iced tea. I'll get chives and basil."

Billy stepped carefully around the plants. "What are we gonna do?"

Noelle stood, stretched, and touched the tip of Billy's nose. "Teach you how to cook . . ."

Jonathan was still asleep, when Noelle, Billy, and Kelly entered the cabin. Kelly ran happily over to sniff and kiss him, but Noelle stopped her.

"Kelly, no. C'mere, little girl. Jonathan has to sleep."

Kelly ran to Noelle, ears back, tail wagging. Noelle led her and Billy to the kitchen area in another corner of the cabin. She put the herbs down on the counter, and smiled, watching Billy imitate her.

Noelle opened the almost empty refrigerator and freezer. She and Billy peered inside.

"Where's all your food?" Billy asked.

"I expected to be at your house for a month, so I ate it."

Billy seriously inspected the freezer. Then he smiled. "There's frozen mini pizzas!"

"Okay," Noelle nodded. "We'll use herbs later. Can you read the pizza instructions?"

"Of course, I can read," Billy said impatiently. "Everybody except stupid people can read."

Billy read the instructions silently, while Noelle talked to him. "Haven't you noticed some of the kids in your class don't read?"

"Yeah. They're stupid. Two minutes in the microwave."

Billy popped six mini pizzas into the microwave, and sat at the kitchen table. He bounced his knees, and tapped his fingers.

Noelle shook her head. "That's not true. They just need special teaching. I knew a man, who didn't learn to read 'til he was 16. When he was your age, they told him he was retarded and a behavior problem, cuz he couldn't sit still."

Billy guiltily stopped drumming the table and bouncing his knee. "What happened to him?"

"They put him into military academy to learn discipline."

"Mom wanted to send me to boarding school. I said, I'd run away."

"That's what this man did. He ran away, joined the circus, and the lion tamer gave him his first book, *The Black Stallion*."

Suddenly, they heard Jonathan's voice. "That was a great book."

"Oh, Jonathan! You're awake!" Noelle approached the bed. Billy and Kelly ran ahead of her to get there first.

"How do you feel, Dad?"

Jonathan used his good arm to touch Billy's face and hair. "No boarding school, Billy."

Billy smiled broadly. "Thanks, Dad."

The microwave beeped. Billy put his shoulders back proudly. "I made lunch!"

Billy and Kelly ran to take out the pizzas. Noelle sat on the side of the bed, checking Jonathan's bandage.

"So, how do you feel?"

"I hurt everywhere."

"Time heals all wounds."

"Early bird gets the worm. Time heals all wounds. You're full of wisdom, Teach."

Billy ran over with the tray of pizzas and some plates. He distributed everything, and bit into his first piece.

"Ow! This is hot!"

Jonathan laughed. "Then blow on it! Let it cool."

They all blew on their pizza. Billy noticed Kelly was drooling. "Look, Kelly is drooling for pizza."

Noelle gave Kelly a bite of crust.

Jonathan was surprised. "I thought Kelly doesn't drool."

Noelle shrugged her shoulders. "I lied. Lucy was being a bitch."

Jonathan chuckled. "Hah! Lucy's the one who drools . . ."

≈

Lucy was indeed drooling, fast asleep, hugging the empty wine bottle to her breast. The stewardess entered, and shook Lucy awake.

"Ms. Weber . . . Ms. Weber . . . You asked me to wake you 30 minutes before we land."

Lucy blinked her eyes several times. "I'm up . . . I'm up! Bring me some coffee and five aspirins!"

Lucy groggily rubbed her forehead, and opened the cocaine vial.

≈

The Topanga General Store was being locked up for the night by its owner, George, while

Dominic read local notices on the store's bulletin board.

A brown station wagon was parked nearby. Louie snored in the passenger seat with his 9mm exposed in his shoulder holster. The cell phone rang.

Louie jumped. "Yeah . . ."

It was Lucy. "Report," she demanded.

"I got nothin'." Louie yawned sleepily. "Manny hasn't called. Me and Dom cruised Topanga. Now we're sittin' outside the General Store. This Noelle Splendor isn't in the phone directory, and we don't wanna ask questions."

"For once, you're thinkin'," Lucy drawled. "No point in some yokel telling her people have been looking for her."

"Lucy, I didn't tell ya that Jonathan, Billy, and the broad saw me."

"Weren't you wearing a mask?"

"Nah. I didn't bring it this morning, cuz we were just takin' ya to the airport."

Lucy furiously stood up. "Louie, with a few more brains, you could've been a half-wit!"

"I'm sorry," Louie said, even though he really wasn't.

"Sorry isn't good enough! This teacher bitch isn't someone we can pay off to forget your face! Now you have to kill them all!"

Louie couldn't believe it. "Even Billy?"

"Whatsa matter? You want some kid looking for you to avenge his father's death? Maybe you should tell him you killed his mother and sister, too! Then he'll really love his Cousin Louie!"

The idea made Louie very uncomfortable. "This is cuttin' into the family pretty deep, Lucy. Why does Vito want to whack Jonathan so bad?"

"Jonathan is an embarrassment," Lucy said simply, "and the family can't afford those. Something for you to remember, Louie! You've got to stay tough, even get tougher, if you're gonna take over after Uncle Vito dies! Now, find that Rolls Royce, and you find them. I want this business done before I get back from New York!"

A stove light showed Billy and Kelly asleep and entwined between Jonathan and Noelle, who were also asleep, but on either end of the bed.

The humans were still dressed. Jonathan moaned in his sleep, awakening Noelle. She checked the clock, and went to kneel beside Jonathan.

Jonathan was crying out in his slumber. "No! No! Leave me alone!"

Noelle spoke to him softly. "Jonathan, wake up. It's just a bad dream."

Jonathan sat up straight. "I didn't do anything wrong!"

Noelle felt his head for fever. "It's okay. You're okay."

Jonathan moved her hand off his head. "What time is it?"

Noelle sat on the floor next to the bed. "A little after midnight."

"I have the same two nightmares. In the first one, I have to save a person, trying to commit suicide. In the second, I'm being chased by a dark figure. It's relentless. I can't escape. That's the one I just had."

"How long have you had these dreams?"

"Since I was Billy's age."

"Did anything traumatic happen to you when you were 10?"

Jonathan stared at her steadily for a moment then decided to trust her. "My mother died."

"That'll do it. I'm sorry."

Jonathan shrugged. "Yeah . . . thanks. I have to pee." He tried to get up, but his pain sent him back down.

Noelle immediately stood up. "Let me help you."

Jonathan allowed Noelle to assist him out of the bed and to the bathroom door. "Wanna help me pee, too?"

"Not tonight, thanks!"

Jonathan went into the bathroom, leaving the door open. Noelle curled up on the bed, watching Billy and Kelly together. Kelly's eyes were open, but Billy remained asleep. Noelle pet Kelly lovingly.

Jonathan spoke to her from the bathroom. "You know what I'd give to have some vodka right now?"

"Nothing that would interest me."

"What does interest you?"

"Contentment." Noelle gently played with Kelly's ears.

Jonathan exited the bathroom, limping to the bay window. "How do you achieve it?"

"It's as easy as looking at Billy and Kelly resting together."

Jonathan did, and smiled. Kelly wagged her tail, and hopped off the bed. Billy stirred.

Noelle carefully stood, so as not to wake him. "Wanna go for a walk with Kelly and me outside?"

He gingerly stretched his muscles. "I'm awfully sore."

Noelle encouraged him. "C'mon. It'll do you good."

A full moon lit the corral. Jonathan and Noelle left the cabin door open so they could hear if Billy awakened, and walked slowly over to Missy the Mare in her stall.

"Kelly and this beautiful horse have taught me how to let go of guilt," Noelle said. "Without that human invention to harass me, I have time for painting, books, sunsets . . ."

"Your paintings are wonderful," Jonathan said, almost shyly.

"Thanks." Noelle blushed. "After seeing the fine art at your house, that's quite a complement."

Together, they petted the mare, who whinnied with delight.

Jonathan tried not to sound too inquisitive. "What finally happened to the man, who taught himself to read with *The Black Stallion*?"

"He became a psychologist who wanted to specialize in leisure."

"Hah! What does that mean?"

"His philosophy was 'Guilt sucks.' He wanted to teach people how to change their lives through enjoying their leisure time, and have his office be a sailboat."

"Sounds like an extraordinary man," Jonathan said with a touch of jealousy.

"I loved him very much, but he died nearly eight years ago from complications of alcoholism."

"Oh, man, I'm sorry. So you know about mourning . . ."

Noelle knelt down to hug Kelly. "Yes, but maybe more importantly for you, I also know about how alcoholism can kill people."

"You got in pretty deep today, Noelle. I owe you."

"No. You owe yourself a better life, although I must admit your environment is pretty complicated."

"Thanks for not asking questions."

Noelle shrugged her shoulders, and stood up. "You'll talk when you're ready."

"Noelle . . . would you hug me? I could really use a hug."

They hugged for a long moment. Jonathan lifted Noelle's chin, and searched her eyes. He leaned in, just about to kiss her, when they heard Billy's voice from inside the cabin.

"Hey, where is everybody?"

Jonathan and Noelle broke their embrace, and walked toward the cabin. Jonathan called out to Billy, while slipping his arm around Noelle's shoulders.

"We're outside on our way in, Billy."

11

The dark roads of Topanga Canyon were lit up by Dominic's headlights. Louie snored on, oblivious to Dominic stopping at a soft shoulder pullout. Dominic shook him.

"Louie, wake up! My turn to sleep."

Louie mumbled, "Five more minutes."

Dominic shoved him. "Bullshit, man! You said that a half hour ago. It's four in the morning! Your turn to drive."

Louie forced himself awake, got out of the car, and walked to the bushes, overlooking the canyon. With his back to Dominic, who moved into the passenger seat, he peed into the bushes.

Louie sighed. "You know, Dom, sometimes I wish I was livin' a different life."

"You and me both, Big Louie. My wife keeps naggin' me, I don't spend enough time at home. At least, I got one, though. Musta been a hard hit for Jonathan to lose his old lady and kid."

"He sure loved 'em," Louie agreed.

"Who wants him whacked, Louie?"

Louie zipped up his fly, and crammed himself into the driver's seat.

"Don't ask questions, Dominic."

≈

The bay window sill was just wide enough for Kelly to lean on it comfortably. While the sun rose, she watched Missy eat leftover alfalfa.

Noelle awakened, and saw Jonathan and Billy still asleep. She joined Kelly, who wagged her tail, and licked Noelle's face. Noelle petted her vigorously.

"Morning, kiddo. How ya doin'? I'm gonna take a shower."

Noelle opened the top half of the Dutch door, letting in the morning sunshine. On the bottom half, she removed a doggie door. Kelly immediately ran outside.

Noelle took clean jeans and a T-shirt out of a chest of drawers. She entered the bathroom, and turned on the shower.

The sound of the running water woke Billy. He tiptoed to the window, saw Kelly chasing birds, and ran out to join her.

The door slammed behind him, which awakened Jonathan. He limped around the room groaning with pain.

Jonathan studied Noelle's paintings, her novels, and her books on art, sailing, philosophy, and psychology. He wondered who this woman really was, and how the hell they were going to get out of the mess they were in.

Jonathan entered the kitchen area, where he saw a jar of coffee beans, a grinder, and a coffee machine, which he promptly turned upside down.

"She's gotta at least have some instant coffee!"

Noelle finished her shower. Drying herself with a giant towel, she wiped off the steam on the medicine cabinet mirror and looked into her own eyes in the reflection.

"I'm okay, they're okay. I'm taking care of myself, no matter what. I'm sailing around the world, and living happily ever after."

≈

Without servants, Jonathan was a fish out of water. Coffee beans were spilled all over the kitchen counter and floor. He cracked an egg into a bowel, but got a bunch of shell into the yolk. His fingers betrayed him, failing to catch any of the shell.

In the bedroom, Noelle dressed leisurely. In the backyard, Billy and Kelly explored secrets only a boy and his dog knew.

And back in the kitchen, a frustrated Jonathan opened a drawer, looking for help with the elusive egg shell. He found a butcher knife.

Using the tip of the oversized knife, Jonathan still couldn't pick up that damned egg shell.

"Shit!" he yelled.

"What's the matter?" Noelle asked, coming up behind him.

Jonathan spun around, and found Noelle in clean clothes, trying to look over his shoulder.

"Don't come in yet," he said, blocking her view. "Billy made lunch, and you made dinner. I thought I'd make breakfast, but . . ."

Jonathan gestured to the mess that he couldn't quite hide.

Noelle tried not to laugh. "You haven't cooked in a while."

"Never. The servants or the women prepared the food."

Noelle walked to the bay window, and saw Billy trying to put a saddle on Missy the Mare, but he wasn't tall enough to do it successfully.

"C'mon," she invited Jonathan. "Let's check on Billy."

They took their time strolling toward the corral. Noelle had her doubts about Jonathan's lack of culinary skills.

"You've really never cooked for yourself?"

"When I was a kid, Myrna used to chase Lucy, Louie, and me out of the kitchen for stealing cookies."

"Cousin Louie? The one who shot you?"

"Yup. Uncle Vito's other nephew."

"It'd really help if you could explain all of this."

"I can't without telling you more than is safe for you to know."

"I think I'm already in danger, Jonathan."

Billy put the heavy saddle down, and he and Kelly ran to greet them. "Hey, what's for breakfast?"

"I tried to make some eggs, but . . ."

"Dad, you tried to cook?"

"Gimme a break, Billy," Jonathan said sheepishly.

Noelle had an idea. "Jonathan, do you feel well enough to go out for breakfast?"

"I feel okay, but I don't think it's a good idea to take the Rolls Royce anywhere. It's too obvious, and your Mini Cooper is back at my house."

"Any minute now, the kid who was gonna feed Missy the Mare, while I was at your house, will be here in a pickup truck. He's a friend, so I think we can borrow his truck if I drop him at home."

Jonathan suddenly got worried, glancing up at the clearing and driveway.

"I don't want anyone to see Billy and me here. They might tell somebody, and in my family, the walls have ears."

Billy chimed in. "Yeah, Noelle. Did you ever see my Dad's surveillance room? It's cool! He's got the whole house bugged!"

Noelle nodded sagely. "I see . . . How about you and Billy keep a low profile 'til I get back from taking Tommy?"

Billy pulled on Jonathan's arm. "Kelly showed me a great place to hide, Dad. C'mon . . ."

<hr/>

Louie parked the station wagon a little ways down the road from the closed Topanga General Store. He got out, slamming the door behind him.

This woke up Dominic, who irritably opened his window to complain. "It can't be time for me to drive!"

"Nah. Go back to sleep," Louie assured him. "Nobody's up this early on Sunday."

Louie walked into the bushes, and zipped down his fly. Just as he started peeing, the cell phone rang in his pocket.

"Damn!" Louie finished a long pee, zipped up his fly, and finally answered the ringing phone.

"Yeah . . ."

Lucy sat in the rear of the limo with her hair back in its tight bun. She snorted cocaine.

"Where the hell were you?" she snapped into the phone.

"Pissing!"

"You can't answer while you piss?!"

"Not unless I get my pants wet!"

Lucy opened the limo's bar, and poured brandy into a steaming cup of coffee. "All right, report!"

Louie reluctantly updated her. "We still haven't found them."

Lucy gulped the too hot coffee, and jumped in her seat. "Fuck, I just burned my tongue!! Did you call that computer guy?"

"I didn't think of it," Louie said. "I don't get this computer shit."

"Do you think at all, you dumb ox? Muscle with no brains! They'll track his credit card purchases!"

Louie paced angrily. He distanced the phone from his ear, but he still heard Lucy yelling at him.

"Do I have to think of everything?!"

Louie was cross. "All right, fine! Let's hang up, so I can call 'em!"

Lucy wasn't done. "I'm flying to L.A. today."

"How come? I thought tomorrow."

"Because you're incompetent, and I finished early. Met with the family last night, and we made the legal strategy for Cousin Santa Claus."

"You want me at the airport?" Louie tried to sound sincere, but Lucy didn't want him anyway.

"No! Stay on Jonathan."

"I need some real sleep, Lucy. Let's put a 100 men on it."

"No! I want as few people as possible involved. Now Topanga's all we've got! Call that computer guy. When I get in, I'll come out and see you."

"I can't wait . . ." Louie said dryly.

Lucy bit. "Do I detect sarcasm?"

"'Course not, baby . . ." Louie said, sounding oily.

"You don't deserve to call me baby!" Lucy hung up on Louie, who angrily folded up his cell phone.

"I oughta dump that bitch!"

Kelly shimmied down into a hole under the cabin. Billy followed her. Jonathan balked.

"I can't fit under there!"

"Sure you can, Dad. There's lotsa space."

Jonathan didn't budge.

Noelle tried to encourage him. "C'mon, Jonathan. I told you, Kelly's not afraid of dark places!"

"But my shoulder . . ."

Noelle heard a car. "Uh oh. Here comes Tommy."

Jonathan immediately scooted under the cabin. Noelle approached the pickup coming into the driveway.

"Hi, Tommy. Happy New Year."

"Happy New Year, Noelle, but what are you doin' here? I thought you were gone."

"Sorry I didn't call you about this morning, but I didn't expect to be here. I still want you to feed Missy 'til you hear from me."

"That's okay, Noelle. I got a bunch of customers in Topanga today, this bein' the holidays and all. Say, where'd you get that Rolls Royce? She's a beauty." Tommy hopped out for a closer look.

Noelle nervously pulled him away. "Oh, it belongs to a friend. Listen, Tommy, I need a favor."

"Sure. What year is the car anyway?"

"I don't know. Tommy, I'm kind of in a hurry. I want to borrow your truck, and have it back to you by dawn tomorrow."

"Well, you were my last stop, but I was gonna get some groceries . . . Unless, of course, you wanna trade the Rolls for the truck."

"Hah! You wish! How 'bout if I give you a ride to the General Store, and I pay George to deliver you and your groceries home?"

"Aw, I can walk from there, Noelle."

"I appreciate this, Tommy." Noelle walked to the truck.

Tommy glanced again at the Rolls. "Great car, Noelle. A real nice sled."

"Listen, Tommy, don't mention it to anyone, okay. My friend wants it to stay low profile."

"Sure, sure. I can keep a secret."

～

The Topanga General Store was open for business. Dominic was asleep in the station wagon parked outside the entrance.

Noelle pulled up in the truck. Tommy hopped out and they waved good-bye.

Tommy entered the store, and saw George, the owner, reading a newspaper.

"Mornin', George. Happy New Year."

"Same to you, Tommy."

"You should see the great Rolls Royce, Noelle Splendor's keepin'."

George snorted. "Too rich for my blood."

"Don't tell anybody, though. She wants to keep it low profile."

Tommy turned into another aisle, bumping right into a smiling Louie.

12

As Noelle parked back at the cabin, and hopped out of the truck, Kelly ran to greet her.

"Hi there, little girl!"

Kelly licked Noelle's face.

Billy raced out of the cabin. "Noelle, c'mere, you gotta see Dad!"

She worriedly rushed inside with Kelly and Billy behind her. Jonathan was dressed as Santa Claus with white beard and hair.

Billy burst out laughing. "Surprise!"

Jonathan patted himself on his cushioned stomach. "Ho, ho, ho! Have you been a good girl?"

Noelle wasn't sure whether to be angry at Billy for scaring her, or laugh at how silly

Jonathan looked. She opted for middle of the road. She was civilized.

"I'm glad you're feeling better, Santa."

Billy couldn't stop bouncing around the room. He had happy feet. "After you left, Dad took a shower, and I cleaned the kitchen. I made frozen orange juice! Want some?"

Noelle drank some of the juice. "Mm. It's delicious, Billy." The little boy beamed with pride.

Jonathan took off the Santa Claus beard and wig. "I couldn't find any clean clothes to fit me except this. How come you have a Santa Claus get up?"

"I go to an orphanage on Christmas Day to entertain the kids. C'mon outside, you guys."

Noelle led Jonathan, Billy, and Kelly to the Rolls Royce. As they walked, Billy sidled up closer to Noelle.

"Where's your family, Noelle?"

"My parents died about ten years ago. My brothers and their families live back east."

Noelle opened the trunk of the Rolls. It was neatly packed with three overnight bags. Joey's gun was on top of one of them.

"Wow! The .357 Magnum!" Billy reached for it, but Jonathan lifted it out first.

"Joey's gun," he said, feeling its weight.

"Yes," Noelle confirmed. "And overnight bags that Manny packed. You can take off the Santa Claus suit for clean shorts, and Billy can shower . . ."

Billy screwed up his nose. Noelle threw him an overnight bag. She grabbed the other bags, and shut the trunk.

Jonathan checked out the gun. "It's loaded."

Noelle smirked. "What a surprise . . ."

≈

Tommy exited the store with several bags of groceries, and started walking home. Louie subtly followed him until he reached the station wagon.

Tommy, of course, kept going, but Louie squeezed his bulk in behind the wheel. He hit Dominic on the arm, jarring him awake. "What?! What is it?"

Louie started the engine, watching Tommy walk up the road. "We got somethin' . . ."

≈

Noelle drove the pickup down Pacific Coast Highway. Jonathan rode shotgun. Billy and Kelly played in the back of the truck next to the overnight bags.

Noelle fiddled with the radio. Jonathan was amused. "Why won't you tell me why we brought the overnight bags with us?"

Noelle kept her eyes on the road. "I like mysteries." She pulled into a parking space in a shopping center.

Jonathan was completely puzzled. "We're eating breakfast here?"

Noelle turned off the motor. "We're gonna make one stop."

Billy started to climb out of the truck, with Kelly right behind him, but Noelle stopped them.

"Billy, Kelly isn't allowed in the mall. Will you keep her company?"

"Sure." Billy settled back into a comfortable position.

Noelle scratched Kelly's ears. "Kelly, stay here. Take care of Billy and the truck."

Kelly wagged her tail, and barked once. Noelle kissed her, and then walked toward the shopping center.

Jonathan followed Noelle. "I'm letting you take the lead, you know."

"Of course, you are." Noelle smiled demurely.

In the men's department, Noelle pulled out Jonathan's wallet. His eyes widened.

"My wallet?!"

"We're paying for your blue jeans."

"My what?!"

"I never saw so many suits in a closet," Noelle said, "but no blue jeans!"

Jonathan was embarrassed. "Not since I was a teenager."

Noelle's eyes twinkled. "Things are about to change."

Tommy whistled as he walked, having no idea he was being tailed by Louie and Dominic. With no one else in sight, Louie pulled up casually in the station wagon.

"Excuse me, kid, how do I get to Sunset Blvd.?"

Tommy walked closer to be heard. "Well, you gotta . . ."

Tommy stopped short, seeing Louie's 9mm, pointing at him. He dropped his groceries, and ran. Louie fired a shot at his thigh.

Tommy fell to the ground, yelling. Louie and Dominic jumped out of the car. Louie grabbed Tommy, and Dominic grabbed the groceries.

Louie opened the back door of the station wagon, and shoved a moaning Tommy inside. Dominic threw the groceries onto the floor.

They jumped back into the car. Louie gunned the motor, and they were gone without anyone to see.

≈

Noelle sat in the blue jeans section of the clothing store. Jonathan came out of a dressing room, wearing jeans, T-shirt, and sneakers.

Noelle was impressed. "You look great!"

Jonathan wasn't sure. He walked to a full length mirror. "I feel like a kid!"

"What's the problem with that?"

"In my business, kids get eaten."

"What is your business?"

Jonathan watched Noelle's reflection in the mirror. He checked out a salesperson, who rang up another customer.

"I told you, criminal law."

"But who is your family?"

Jonathan's head darted around to see if anyone was coming. He walked to Noelle, bending down on one knee next to her chair.

"Noelle . . . let's just say, they are influential, wealthy people, who represent other influential, wealthy people, who are charged with criminal activity."

"Hah! It sounds like the Mob!"

"Shhh!!!" Jonathan's eyes searched everywhere.

Noelle spoke in a normal volume. "C'mon, Jonathan, the Mob only happens to people in the movies!"

Jonathan put his hand over Noelle's mouth, shaking his head no. He slowly took his hand away, and Noelle whispered, "The Mafia?! The Mob?!!"

Jonathan nodded yes, checking over his shoulder again.

Noelle spoke softly. "Does Billy know?"

Jonathan whispered, "I don't think so. He knows we play some pretty funky games with stuff like the surveillance equipment . . . and now Cousin Louie shooting at us . . . but I don't think he connects us to . . ."

". . . the source?" Noelle supplied.

Jonathan nodded yes.

Noelle furrowed her brow. "I need to rethink this . . ."

Jonathan laughed out loud, standing and stretching his arms.

"I've already been thinking, my sweet Noelle. They have connections to the ends of the Earth! There is nowhere on the planet to hide!"

Jonathan saw the salesperson approaching. "May I help you, sir?"

Jonathan pointed at Noelle. "She's in charge."

Noelle pulled out Jonathan's wallet. She opened it, revealing a selection of credit cards. She rifled through the cash.

"Any preferences, Jonathan, on how I pay for this?"

Jonathan quipped, "Yeah, use your money! I'd like to save mine for . . . emergencies!"

Noelle thought about this. "Hmm. Let's conserve your cash."

Noelle picked a shiny credit card, handed it to the salesperson, and then suddenly grabbed it back from the surprised employee.

"Jonathan, were you kidding me?"

"No."

Noelle turned back to the salesperson. "Uh, we'll use cash instead . . ."

≈

The station wagon was parked on a bluff. Louie and Dominic held Tommy near the edge. His injured leg bled through his pants.

Louie was practically pleading with him. "C'mon, Tommy, you don't want to go over the side . . ."

Tommy was shaken, but not stirred. "If you drop me over the side, you'll never find out!"

Louie sighed, looking at Dominic. "These kids today are smart."

Dominic nodded. "The MTV generation . . ."

≈

At the shopping center, Jonathan and Noelle exited the store, and walked back to the truck.

Jonathan was curious. "What was with the credit card?"

Noelle was quite proud of herself. "I saw it in a movie once, where a computer tracked this guy through his credit card purchases."

"So you believe me?!"

"Yes. We need a plan, Butch."

Billy waved from the truck, and Kelly wagged her tail. "Cool jeans, Dad!"

"Thanks, Billy."

"I'm getting' pretty hungry, Noelle."

"No more interruptions, Billy Boy."

≈

Dominic drove the brown station wagon, watching Louie and Tommy in the rear view mirror.

Louie tried another approach. "How old are ya, kid?"

Tommy was working hard on staying composed. "Seventeen."

"Okay, so you're old enough to know I could hurt you real bad if I wanted to . . ."

Tommy pushed his hands down on his thigh to stop the bleeding.

"Then you must not want to. C'mon, Mister, let me go. I told Noelle I would keep the car low profile, and I meant it."

Louie sighed deeply, moving his beefy muscle closer to Tommy. Tommy moved closer to the door. Louie flipped the master lock switch. All the door locks snapped down. Tommy's eyes widened.

Louie's voice became more menacing. "Now, just because I don't want to hurt you, don't mean I won't."

Louie took out his gun, and pointed it at Tommy's bloody thigh. "I shot ya, right?"

Tommy's breathing was labored. "Yeah . . ."

"I could shoot you again . . ."

Tommy inched back, trying to disappear into the seat. "Please, don't shoot me again! You wouldn't rat on a friend, Mister, would ya? You wouldn't!"

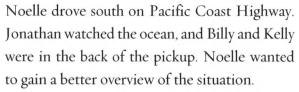

13

Noelle drove south on Pacific Coast Highway. Jonathan watched the ocean, and Billy and Kelly were in the back of the pickup. Noelle wanted to gain a better overview of the situation.

"So, you work for these guys, and you're related?"

"My mother was Uncle Vito's sister. My father is *consigliere*, and I'm next in line."

"Let me guess . . . you want out?"

"Uncle Vito doesn't want the family to get too far away."

"What about vacations?"

"He wants us to stay in contact. A transmitter is surgically implanted into our brains, like James Bond put underneath cars, when he wanted to track them . . ."

". . . What?!"

"I'm kidding! I'm kidding! But only about the transmitter!"

Noelle rolled her eyes. "Now, I don't know what to believe!"

Jonathan turned serious. "Well, you know the bullet Louie shot at me was real. My family really is . . . the family!"

Noelle exited the Pacific Coast Highway in Santa Monica.

"Are we gonna eat in Santa Monica?" Jonathan asked.

"Marina Del Rey."

"What's there?"

"Boats."

"Uh-uh. I get seasick!"

"Then you'll thank modern medicine . . ."

～

A stalemate existed between Louie and Tommy in the brown station wagon. Dominic lost his patience.

"You're too soft, Louie. I bet Tommy wants to know what'll happen if he don't get to a doctor."

Louie nodded. "'Dis is a good point. You ain't been shot before, have you, kid?"

A terrified Tommy shook his head no.

Louie continued. "Your body don't like havin' a bullet inside. So, it gets a fever, and infected, and you die!"

Louie used his gun to nudge Tommy's hand away from his wound. Blood oozed. Tommy quickly put his hand back, pushing hard.

Louie persisted. ". . . Or you could bleed to death."

Tommy cried out, "You don't want me dead!"

Louie agreed. "True, kid. But it'll take a while, and watchin' people die is somethin' I've done before."

Dominic put in his two cents. "It ain't pretty, Tommy."

Tommy breathed hard, looking back and forth between the men.

"On the other hand," Louie reasoned, "I could rip up your pants, and make a pressure bandage. That'd hold you 'til we get to Noelle's. She'll know a doc . . ."

Tommy licked his lips. He wanted to tell them.

Louie played him like a fishing line. He let out a little more bait. "I just wanna talk to her, Tommy. I'm not gonna hurt her . . ."

Tommy studied Louie's eyes. He took a deep breath.

"You're lying . . ."

Louie chuckled, and shook his head from side to side. "You got balls, kid."

The brilliance of the sunny day in Marina Del Rey shone on the water and the boats. Noelle yelled out the window to Billy.

"Billy, do you want to eat breakfast on a sailboat?"

Billy raised his fist to the sky. "Yes!"

Jonathan complained. "Now he's gonna be disappointed, because I won't go on a boat!"

Noelle decided to smile at him, rather than frown. "You don't like boats, or water?"

Jonathan crossed his arms in front of him, staring outside. "Water. I . . . I can't swim."

Noelle kindly touched Jonathan's arm. "I have life preservers."

Jonathan practically pouted. "I want to go to a regular restaurant . . . one with a bar! Boats and water make me thirsty!"

Noelle laughed, and searched for a parking space between two basins. She tried to distract him with conversation.

"Why does Uncle Vito want you dead?"

"I started drinking heavily around the time they made me a full partner in the law firm. That's when I found out who we are."

"Heavy drinking hardly seems like a reason to put out a contract."

"They're afraid I might talk to the Feds when I'm drunk."

"I take it you've considered it."

"Yeah, but I know the family can get to somebody in the witness protection program. With enough time and money, anybody can be gotten to."

"I'm surprised they didn't try putting you in a rehab hospital."

"They did. Six months ago. But then at Jenny's fifth birthday party, I got so depressed thinking about the dismal future I could offer her, that I got really drunk. Melinda had been dipping into the wine, and we got into an ugly fight. When the muscle men tried to remove us, I broke some furniture."

"The kids must have been terrified."

"I remember Jenny beating her little fists on this huge mother fucker, saying, 'Let my Daddy go. He didn't do anything to you!'"

Jonathan viciously pounded his fist onto the dashboard. "She didn't deserve to get hurt!"

"Nobody does! There isn't any right or wrong, Jonathan. Things just are the way they are. How'd you do at the rehab?"

"Melly stayed, but I . . . I escaped."

Noelle laughed, pulling into a parking space. "You're about to escape again!"

Jonathan shook his head firmly. "I'm not going on a boat!

Kelly led the way for Billy, and they both jumped onto a beautiful 40 foot sailboat called 'Noelle's Ark.' Noelle unlocked the cabin, and Jonathan lagged behind.

Billy was ecstatic. "Wow, 'Noelle's Ark!' Is she really yours?"

"One hundred percent," Noelle said proudly.

Jonathan was in the mood to be skeptical. "You do pretty well for yourself. A horse and a sailboat?"

"I don't own Missy the Mare," Noelle explained. "I just rent that cabin, and the man who owns it, lets me ride Missy if I take care of her. I like simplicity. Actually, I'm a low maintenance person."

"And I want to be low profile," Jonathan said thoughtfully.

"Exactly. Come aboard. I could use a crew."

Jonathan didn't get the whole picture yet. "What are you talking about?"

Noelle threw Jonathan a small box. He took out two gray wristbands. "What are these?"

"Prevents seasickness with a bead to make pressure points on each of your wrists."

Billy and Kelly ran the length of the boat. "How big is she, Noelle?"

"Forty feet."

Jonathan read the instructions, playing with the wristbands.

"What do you mean, you need a crew?"

"The doc and I were going to follow the sun. Sail the seven seas."

"That plan changed."

"Correct. Since he died, I've bought and sold a few sailboats, getting a bigger one each time. I can't single hand a 40 footer easily on a long distance trip. I'm not strong enough."

"You could hire anybody."

"I don't want to sail around the world with anybody."

"But we just met you! This is crazy! I can't even swim!"

Noelle lifted up a seat in the cockpit, taking out a life preserver. She threw it to Jonathan, who caught it.

"You'll learn."

"Is this breakfast or kidnapping?"

"Hah! Breakfast!"

Billy and Kelly ran over to stand next to Noelle. "C'mon, Dad. Grandpa says, practice dying!"

Jonathan didn't get it. "What's that supposed to mean?"

Noelle said, "I read that when Socrates was on his deathbed, a student asked what was the most important thing he'd learned. The great teacher said, 'Practice dying!'"

Billy also had an explanation. "Grandpa says, live everyday like it's our last, and we'll be happy."

"Well, Grandpa never told me that," Jonathan said, sounding insulted.

"Maybe you weren't listening," Noelle suggested.

Jonathan cocked his head to one side, then abruptly got on the boat.

Billy yelled, "Yay!" and hugged Jonathan very tightly. Noelle smiled at him over Billy's shoulders.

≈

Dominic stopped the brown station wagon at a soft shoulder pullout. Louie softly slapped and shook a nearly unconscious Tommy.

"C'mon, kid, where does Noelle live? We can get this bullet outta you there. Tell me, Tommy!"

"Please, Mister . . . A doctor . . ."

"Noelle will know one, but we don't know how to get to her house!"

Tommy took a deep breath, and finally gave in. "Go back to the General Store . . . I'll direct you from there."

Louie immediately ripped off a strip of Tommy's pants, making a pressure bandage for the bloody thigh. Dominic made a U-turn.

≈

Breakfast in the cockpit was coming to a close. Jonathan, Noelle, and Billy basked in the sun while finishing their meal.

Billy burped. "You make a mean omelet, Noelle."

Noelle laughed. "Thanks, Billy."

Jonathan commented, "You're awfully nice to Noelle, Billy."

Billy shrugged. "She's nice to me."

Noelle smiled. "You catch more flies with honey than vinegar!"

Jonathan shook his head. "More pearls of wisdom . . ." He stood, lifting his empty plate. He motioned to Billy, and said, "Billy and I will do the dishes."

Simultaneously, Billy and Jonathan reached for Noelle's plate. They each tried to take it, jealously playing tug o'war.

Noelle jumped up. "It's okay! I'll wash. Jonathan, you can dry. Billy, how about fishing here in the harbor?"

"Maybe I can catch lunch!"

"That's the spirit! Follow me!"

Kelly followed everybody inside the cabin. Noelle pointed to the fishing gear. Billy grabbed a rod, and the lure box.

Jonathan was surprised. "You know what to do?"

"Sure. Grandpa Martin taught me."

"Where was I during all these Grandpa Martin events?"

"You used to sleep a lot, Dad."

"Vodka will do that," Noelle added.

Jonathan sheepishly hugged Billy. "Go fishin', kid. I'll join you in a little bit."

"You want to go now?" Noelle asked. "I can dry."

"No," Jonathan said. "I'd just as soon talk."

Noelle nodded, and started the dishes. When Billy and Kelly exited, she and Jonathan started to speak simultaneously. They both said, "So . . ."

Embarrassed and laughing, they both said, "Go ahead. No, you."

Noelle insisted, "No, really. You go ahead."

Jonathan said, "All right. Did you marry the psychologist?"

Noelle handed him a dish. "No. His name was Jimmy, and he had an awful divorce behind him. I always figured the best way to not get divorced was to not get married."

Jonathan dried the dish. "Sounds reasonable."

Noelle nodded. "I think so, but we were common law married for 20 years, so I think of him as my husband."

"Hey, how come your boat has food on it?" Jonathan asked.

"There's a plug on the dock for the refrigerator, and I like to stay stocked . . . . Just in case I want to make a quick getaway!"

Jonathan laughed nervously. Suddenly, they heard Billy yell.

"Hook up! Hook up!"

Billy's fishing rod was bent over double, when Jonathan and Noelle ran into the cockpit. Jonathan leaned over the side to look in the water.

"I see color!" he shouted.

Noelle ran to Billy's other side. Kelly wagged her tail excitedly. Billy proudly reeled in a hand sized perch. Noelle hugged him.

"All right, Billy! A perch!"

"Lunch!" Billy said, holding up his prize.

"For one of us anyway," Noelle said. "I'll get a bucket of water. It's time to shove off, and get under sail!"

Jonathan wasn't prepared for that progression. "Wait a minute! Let's discuss this!"

Noelle opened a cockpit bench, and reached in for a bucket. "You want a committee meeting?"

"Well . . . yes!" Jonathan conceded.

Noelle hopped off the boat, and took the bucket to a hose. She filled it with water, and on the way back to the boat, she pulled out a plug from a socket. Billy put his fish into the bucket.

Noelle took a count. "Okay, Billy, how do you vote?"

"I vote yes! A thousand times yes!"

Noelle nodded. "Kelly, wanna go sailing?"

Kelly barked and wagged her tail. Billy clapped his hands. Jonathan waved his arms in protest.

"Hey, now, wait a minute . . ."

Noelle interrupted him. "You're outvoted! Crew, cast off!"

≈

Dominic parked the station wagon near Noelle's mailbox.

Tommy said weakly, "This is it . . ."

Louie tapped Dominic on the shoulder. "Dom, go check it out. Hurry, this kid's bleedin' like a sieve."

Dominic opened his door, and made sure his gun was ready. Louie spotted the gun, and said sternly, "No! I don't want you shootin' anybody. Just check it out!"

≈

Honey, can you hear me?

Of course, Noelle.

I feel so strange. Alone, and yet not lonely. Wanting to cry, and yet there are no tears. I thought I would be happier or sleeping better by the time I reached this part of the book, but there's an emptiness knowing that it's all fantasy.

It's not all fantasy, honey. Your memories are real.

But I'm making everything up now, as I go along.

Isn't that what life is all about anyway? Keep writing . . .

≈

14

Jonathan cinched up his life preserver. Noelle guided the boat out of the harbor into the ocean.

"I'm gonna turn into the wind. You guys can raise the main sail."

Billy said, "But how do we do that?"

To Billy's and Noelle's surprise, Jonathan answered, "I'll show you . . ."

Jonathan unwrapped the main sail, smiling broadly. "How could a Los Angeles native not know how to sail? C'mon, Billy, help me."

Noelle turned the boat into the wind, so Jonathan and Billy could pull up the sail. When they were done, Noelle instructed, "Okay, now the jib sail."

Jonathan showed Billy how to set up the jib. Once they were under sail, Noelle turned off the motor. They enjoyed the gentle rocking of the ocean. Billy and Kelly checked out the forepeak, leaving Noelle and Jonathan in the cockpit.

"When did you learn to sail, Jonathan?"

"As a teenager," Jonathan replied. "One of my friend's fathers had a wooden sailboat."

"You have friends?" Noelle smiled mischievously.

Jonathan wasn't insulted, but he answered seriously. "Had them. It seems like a long time ago. What about you?"

"My friends were Jimmy's friends. When he died . . . I drifted." The water lapped against the side of the boat. "'Don't linger in desolate ground.' *The Art of War*. A small book that packs a powerful punch."

"I've read it," Jonathan said. "It also says, some ground is not to be contested . . ."

"Is that your way of saying, we should let ourselves be killed?" Noelle asked.

"Nobody's trying to kill you," Jonathan reminded her.

"I disagree," Noelle said. "I saw Louie's face, Jonathan. He has to take me out, or risk I turn him into the cops."

Jonathan shook his head, and turned his hands into fists. "So what do we do?"

"When in death ground . . . fight!"

≈

Lucy's airplane came in for a landing. A limo waited for her on the Tarmac. She exited the plane, entered the limo, snorted coke, and dialed the phone, all while her bags were put in the trunk by her new chauffeur.

Louie's knee bounced nervously as he sat next to an unconscious Tommy. His phone rang. Louie answered.

"Yeah."

Lucy barked in his ear. "Report!"

Louie jumped, but gave her the information. "We found her place."

"Bravo, Big Louie. Where?"

"Dominic's seein' if they're home."

"If not, we wait. Now, where . . ."

"I think we're wastin' our time, Lucy."

"Louie, you're going overboard thinking. You're workin' without tools. Now, where are you?"

"3421 Topanga Canyon Blvd."

"Okay! I've got one errand. Then, I'm stopping at Jonathan's house before I come out there. I'm not sure where Manny's loyalty is. Call me if they show. Bye . . ."

". . . but, Lucy . . ."

Lucy had already hung up.

Dominic ran back to the car, sticking his head in the window. "There's nobody there, but a horse."

Tommy piped up. "Missy the Mare . . ."

Louie said, "Okay, drive us down. We'll break in, and wait for 'em. Maybe we can take this bullet out."

"But if we park in there," Dominic said, "they'll see the car when they come back."

"Okay, then just drop us off, and come back after you hide it! I gotta try and help this kid!"

Dominic shook his head in fondness for Louie. "You ain't as tough as you used to be, Big Louie."

Louie shrugged defensively. "Yeah, well . . . nothin' stays the same!"

At the wheel, Jonathan heeled the boat over on its side. Noelle and Billy yelled with delight. Kelly relished the wind.

Lucy's limo sped along, stopping at a liquor store.

Louie gingerly removed the bullet from Tommy's thigh with Noelle's hemostat. Tommy moaned, and Dominic watched the operation intently.

Now Billy was at the wheel, and he sailed into a red sunset, gracing the sky. Jonathan and Noelle sat with him in the cockpit. Kelly stretched out nearby.

Noelle recited a poem. "'Red sky at night, Sailor's delight . . .'"

Billy finished it for her. "'Red sky in morning, Sailor take warning!' Grandpa knows that poem, too!"

Noelle smiled. "Your grandpa sounds like my kind of guy."

Jonathan doesn't get this. "Yeah. He's friendly enough now with Billy, but where was he when I was 10?"

"In mourning," Noelle said. "Didn't you tell me your mother died when you were 10?"

Jonathan nodded. "I never thought of it that way."

"The ocean helps us relax enough to see things differently," Noelle commented.

Billy sighed contentedly. "I love it out here, Dad. I wish we could sail forever!"

Jonathan and Noelle exchanged glances. "What about school, Billy?"

Before Billy could answer, Noelle chimed in. "I'm a credentialed teacher . . ."

Billy jumped up and down, eliciting barking from Kelly. "Could we, Dad? Could we sail around the world? ...May we?"

Jonathan laughed. "Just like that . . . Leave tomorrow?"

Billy was totally confident. "Sure! Why not?"

Jonathan wished he had that kind of confidence. He touched Billy's head affectionately. "Wouldn't you miss the family?"

"Grandpa will visit and fish with us!"

"I wish it were that easy, son."

"It can be," Noelle offered.

Jonathan shook his head, sighing desolately. He stood, and took the wheel from Billy. They all watched the sun sink into the water. As it got darker, Noelle got the chills.

"It's getting cold. I think we better head back to safe harbor."

Jonathan was in a dark mood. "There's no such place . . . Crew, prepare to come about!"

≈

Manny opened the front door to admit Lucy. She waltzed past him, heading for the stairway.

"Manny, help bring in my suitcases. Put the liquor store bag in the refrigerator, but take out the brandy first. Have Inga bring me a snifter, and draw me a bath."

Manny grimaced behind Lucy's back. "Yes, Ms. Weber."

Lucy stopped on the stairs, casually looking over her shoulder. "Has Jonathan called?"

Manny didn't skip a beat. "No, ma'am." Manny exited.

Lucy cocked her head to one side thoughtfully.

≈

The sky was dark except for the moonlight. With sails down, and motor chugging, Jonathan guided the sailboat into its slip in the harbor.

Noelle jumped off at the dock, carrying the dock lines with her. As she tied off the boat, Billy positioned the rubber fenders.

The deflated sailors walked to the pickup, and this time, Jonathan drove. He took them through Marina Del Rey with Noelle riding shotgun. In the back of the truck, Billy nestled into Kelly's warm fur.

Noelle fiddled with the radio, finding a news station. Just as she leaned back into her seat, Jonathan shut off the radio.

"There wouldn't be family visits."

"Even your father?"

"If he knew where we were, Vito could get it out of him."

"Jonathan, what if it's not Vito, who wants you dead? I thought your father told me you had 30 days to get sober."

"Vito gave his word he wouldn't order me hurt before that, but he's a killer, and killers lie."

"Everybody lies, Jonathan. Why would Louie want you dead?"

"Louie's just taking orders."

"Who else does he listen to?"

"My father and Lucy."

Jonathan and Noelle had a simultaneous realization. They both shouted, "Lucy!"

Noelle didn't want to believe it. "Would Lucy be that demented?"

"When I was seven, she hog-tied me, and left me in front of a hearth."

Noelle shivered. "How did you get out of it?"

"I don't remember. I was really fucked up by it. I was screaming. Somebody must have cut me loose."

"But you don't remember if it was Lucy, or if someone rescued you?"

"I remember who did it . . . going up to the pain . . ."

"The pain? Did you get burned?"

"Are you kidding? I almost died! I was hog-tied, staying in the same orientation up against a lit fire!"

"How horrible! We've gotta figure this out, Jonathan!"

"I've thought and thought, Noelle! Even if it is Lucy, even if I sobered up . . ."

"You are sober, nearly 48 hours."

Jonathan cocked his head, smiling at Noelle. "Even if I stayed sober, my work . . . my life is with Vito."

"You're underestimating your brain."

"You have more guts than brains! You don't know how wild I was! Do you think I've gone through some kind of miraculous change in the three days I've known you?"

"There's no magic cure, but I think you have an awareness now that . . ."

". . . That what? That I'm a loser!"

Noelle emphatically shook her head. "No. I see you as a 50 year old male, who needs to dry out from alcohol long enough, to become a self-sufficient leisure loving human."

Jonathan laughed. "You mean my work is just starting."

Noelle nodded. "Think of this sailing adventure as an alternative to a rehab. Jonathan, I know leisure psychology can work! The ocean is Mother Nature rocking you back to sanity. Jimmy and I wanted to take people on extended trips. It would give them the chance to dry out, and take the time to regroup. Reevaluate. Learn new behaviors."

"Why didn't it work for Jimmy?"

"While he was alive, we were both drinking too much, and I smoked a lot of pot. We never got clean and sober together long enough to create a stable life for ourselves."

"You're an alcoholic also, Noelle?"

"Yes. As hard as it still is for me to say that, I know that I can't drink. I have an allergy to alcohol than can kill me."

Jonathan digested this information slowly. "How long has it been since you've had a drink?"

"Three and a half years. If I can do it, you can do it."

"But, Noelle, sailing around the world isn't an afternoon in the sun . . . It would take a couple of years! And besides . . ." Jonathan looked out the window. "We'd be checking over our shoulders the whole time!"

"Listen, Jonathan, with Louie or Lucy or Vito, or somebody trying to kill us, we don't have a lot of options!"

Jonathan eyes remained glued to the road. His silence infuriated Noelle. "Okay, forget it! You're right. We better go our separate ways! Stop the car!"

"What?!"

But Noelle was adamant. "Just do it!"

≈

15

Jonathan pulled over to the side of the road in front of the Marina. Noelle hopped out, and he followed her.

Billy and Kelly alerted to the stop. Billy sleepily lifted his head over the side of the truck. "What's goin' on?"

"Nothing," Noelle said. "Go back to sleep. I'm gonna drive."

Billy slid back down. Noelle's purposeful walk to the driver's side was impeded by Jonathan, who gently pushed her back onto the sidewalk in front of a row of sailboats.

"What are you talking about, Noelle?"

"I'll take you to your house. We'll deal with the demons chasing us independently. I'll be damned, if I'll beg anybody to go sailing! I thought we had fun today!"

"We did!"

Jonathan tried to take Noelle in his arms, but she resisted. "I'm not proposing, Jonathan. I want you to crew my boat. I'll trade my services as a teacher to you and your son. He needs to learn the three little r's, and you need to learn the big R!"

"What's that?"

"RELAX!! Maybe around the world won't happen! We could sail to Mexico, taking one day at a time. It's January. They're catching marlin in Cabo San Lucas."

Billy popped up from the back of the pickup. "Marlin! Dad, she's makin' you an offer you can't refuse!"

Jonathan and Noelle's eyes met, and they burst out laughing.

Noelle's excitement was contagious. "If we do well in Mexico, we can sail to a sequel in Hawaii! Jonathan, I've got almost enough money saved for me to live without working. You know, my father always said I learned things the hard way, but damn it, I've paid my dues, and I've learned the only way to predict the future, is to create the future!"

Jonathan began to consider the idea. "Hmmm, I've got plenty of money . . . just no access to it in a lump sum."

"What do you mean?"

"When we were children receiving money as gifts, Father and Uncle Vito were signers on our accounts. When we became teenagers, they were afraid we might blow it on something stupid. Uncle Vito or my father has to authorize a withdrawal larger than $10,000."

"Why didn't you tell them, hands off, when you turned 21?"

"Hah! You haven't met Uncle Vito."

"Maybe it's time I did."

"Noelle, you don't want to fuck with the dragon . . ."

"I've gotten past dragons before." She shivered. "It's freezing out here. Let's drive while we talk."

"I'll drive . . . to your house!"

Noelle smiled. "All right. We're back on line."

Lines of cocaine were being formed by Lucy, who used a razor blade to divvy up the white powder that sat on a mirror, which was placed on a tray that spanned the width of the tub in the master bathroom of Jonathan's house.

Lucy used a cut straw to inhale the drug. Then she settled back, stretching out her long legs, and resting her head, with her eyes closed.

≈

Jonathan drove the pickup on Pacific Coast Highway.

Noelle argued a point. "I don't understand why you can't simply tell Vito you're leaving. He's not gonna send an army after you. He's a businessman, and it's not cost efficient. He's bluffing, if he says otherwise."

"Noelle, my mother didn't just die. She shot herself. I'm the one who found her body. She'd dressed herself up nice, laid down on the bed, and used a pillow at her head, so she didn't splash anything. Then she blew her brains out."

Noelle's brow wrinkled, and she gently squeezed Jonathan's arm. "Between your mother's suicide, and Lucy hog-tying you, it's no wonder you have your nightmares."

"Mother told me she had been married once before my father. The man beat her, and Uncle Vito had him killed. Then he wouldn't let her out unchaperoned 'til she met my father."

"Your father is a nice man."

Jonathan nodded his agreement. "I'm beginning to think so. Anyway, once he became *consigliere*, my mother got very sad. He always worked, and she always drank. She would hold my hand, and talk to me with tears streaming down. She'd say, don't let them touch you inside, Johnny. Don't let them get you . . ."

Noelle blinked away tears. She clasped fingers with Jonathan. "I wish there were some evidence that would ensure our safety."

"There's nothing," Jonathan said. "I've thought and thought . . . Hey, wait a minute . . ."

Noelle perked up while she watched Jonathan think something through. "The day of Melly's funeral, when Lucy thought I was sleeping, she whispered she'd overheard Uncle Vito and my father talking."

"What were they talking about?"

"That Lucy would be the next *consigliere* if something happened to me."

"That's it then. Lucy must want you dead."

"But the important part is she overheard them. How did she do that? Uncle Vito would shit if he found out Lucy was bugging him."

"Where were they when she heard them?"

"My house . . . MY HOUSE!" Jonathan suddenly pulled into the U-turn lane.

"Where are you going?" Noelle wanted to know.

Jonathan made a wildly fast U-turn. "To get some evidence!"

≈

At Jonathan's house, Lucy came down the stairs into the foyer. She wore a black turtleneck, black pants, and carried a black shoulder bag. Her hair was in its tight bun.

Lucy called out shrilly, "MANNY!"

A moment passed in which she rapidly tapped her foot, and impatiently checked her watch.

"MANNY! INGA!"

Manny entered, his eyes narrow with anger. "Yes, Ms. Weber . . ."

Lucy ripped right into him. "Don't cop an attitude with me, Manny . . ."

Lucy reached into her bag, pulled out a 9mm automatic, and pointed it at Manny, who stiffened visibly.

". . . or you'll be off my crew as fast as I can pull this trigger!"

"I . . . I . . . apologize, Ms. Weber. I appreciate your arranging for my early prison dismissal, and giving me this job."

Lucy threw the gun to Manny, who caught it clumsily.

"Good answer. You might need that if Jonathan shows up. Don't forget whose side you're on. Bring his jeep around to the front with the liquor store bag in it. I'm gonna take a little ride."

≈

Christmas lights still lit Jonathan's street. He drove the pickup down the familiar territory. Just as Lucy pulled out of the gate in his jeep, the pickup cruised toward it.

Jonathan saw the jeep, and immediately braked the truck. He pulled over to the side, and ducked, pushing Noelle down as well.

Jonathan whispered, "That's Lucy in my jeep."

Lucy didn't notice the pickup, and continued to drive away. Jonathan waited until she was out of sight, then parked in front of the gate.

"You, Billy, and Kelly, wait here," he said to Noelle.

"But, Jonathan . . ." she protested.

"I'll be faster alone."

As Jonathan exited the truck, Billy and Kelly stuck their heads over the side in back.

Billy whispered, "Dad?"

Jonathan approached Billy, and tousled his hair. "It's okay, son. I'll be right back. Take care of things."

Billy nodded. Jonathan took Billy's face in his hands, and kissed his forehead. Billy reached around him for a hug. Kelly licked Jonathan's cheek.

As Jonathan broke away to go, Noelle called out, "You'll need these . . ."

She threw Jonathan his key ring. He saluted her, and ran into the darkness.

Jonathan cautiously used his keys to open the security gate. He ran to the front door, and quietly let himself into the house.

Oblivious to the intrusion, Manny, Inga, and Myrna watched TV in the kitchen.

Jonathan felt his way through the moonlit house to the library. He quickly let himself into the surveillance room.

Checking over his shoulder to make sure no one was coming, he flipped on the light, and rapidly sorted through the stack of videotapes.

In the kitchen, Manny stood and stretched his arms. When his jacket flapped open, the 9mm was visible tucked inside his belt. He quickly closed his jacket before Inga or Myrna saw the gun.

Jonathan grabbed the 'Library' videotape, and turned off the light. He peeked into the foyer from the library. Nothing. He ran to the front door, quietly opening it.

Just as Jonathan was about to step outside, he heard Manny's deep voice. "Mr. Weber . . ."

Jonathan turned to see Manny shakily pointing the 9mm right at his heart. Jonathan put up his hands.

"You don't have to do this, Manny. I know you're capable, but I don't think you want to kill me."

"Your sister can be very persuasive."

"You could pack your bags and leave. Get out while you can. That's what I'm trying to do."

Manny drew the hammer back on the 9mm. CLICK . . .

Jonathan edged closer to outside. They locked eyes for a long moment.

Then Manny released the hammer, and lowered the gun. "I'm a forger . . . not a killer."

Jonathan nodded to Manny, and disappeared into the night.

≈

Lucy drove the jeep down Pacific Coast Highway, and turned into Topanga Canyon.

≈

Louie turned on a lamp in Noelle's cabin.

Dominic searched the kitchen. "This Noelle has like no food here!"

Louie loosened his collar. "I could sure use a beer . . ."

≈

Lucy parked the jeep down the road from Noelle's mailbox. She exited the car, carrying a grocery bag, a gift wrapped box, and her shoulder bag.

Lucy stealthily approached the cabin, going around to the backyard. She sneaked in quietly, and saw Missy the Mare. Lucy whispered, "Shh. Nice horsie . . ."

Lucy ducked down, peeking through the bay window. She saw Louie checking on Tommy. Dominic chewed gum, and watched TV.

Louie wiped the sweat off Tommy's brow, then felt his forehead. "It's takin' a long time for his fever to go down. Maybe the bullet was in him too long."

Dominic still watched TV, and talked without looking at Louie. "You're turnin' into Florence Nightin'gale, Big Louie. He's just another cockroach . . ."

Dominic cracked his gum. Louie lumbered to the Dutch door. "Maybe he's sweatin' cuz it's so fuckin' hot! Man, I wish I had a cold beer!"

Louie pulled open the back door, and was scared out of his wits to see Lucy's dark figure, leering at him. He yelled, "Ahhhhhh!"

Dominic jumped, fumbling for his gun. "What?! What is it?!"

Lucy laughed uproariously at her two Keystone cops, but Louie was pissed. "Jesus Christ, Lucy, you scared the shit outta me!"

Lucy pulled a six pack of beer out of the grocery bag. "Did I hear you ask for a cold beer?"

≈

Jonathan spoke animatedly to Noelle, as he drove the pickup down Pacific Coast Highway, and turned into Topanga.

". . . so if I'm right, Lucy is on this videotape eavesdropping."

"I think we're ready to fuck with the dragon," Noelle said.

≈

16

Lucy opened a bottle of wine in Noelle's kitchen. The gift wrapped box stood on the counter. Tommy moaned in his sleep, and Lucy walked to the bed, drinking straight from the bottle of wine as she went.

"Why'd you let the kid live?"

Louie chugged a beer. "I've been thinkin', Lucy . . ."

"I can smell the rubber burning, Louie!" Lucy turned to Dominic. "Dominic, why didn't you kill him?"

Dominic also drank a beer, and he sat nervously in front of Lucy. "I take orders from Louie," he volunteered.

Lucy swigged her wine. "At least, we got somebody who knows how to take orders!"

Lucy examined the kitchen. She opened cabinets, and left them open. She drank more wine, and began opening drawers. She discovered the butcher knife.

Lucy took it out, brandishing it. "Oooh, pretty!"

Lucy used the knife to open more cabinets and drawers. She took the knife with her as she moved around the cabin. She reached one of Noelle's paintings, and took a gulp of her wine.

"Quite the little artist . . ."

Lucy used the butcher knife to viciously slice a jagged cut in the painting. Louie and Dominic jumped. Lucy opened Noelle's chest of drawers. She used the tip of the butcher knife to lift up bikini panties, and fling them on the floor.

Lucy opened Noelle's closet, and found the Santa Claus suit and wig, which was hanging on the inside of the door. She used the tip of the butcher knife to lift up the wig and twirl it.

"Ho, ho, ho . . ." Lucy snarled.

Jonathan turned in at Noelle's mailbox, and parked in the clearing. Billy and Kelly jumped out of the back as Jonathan and Noelle stepped out of the truck.

Billy threw them their overnight bags, and they all walked toward the front door.

"Let's go in the back way so we can say hi to Missy," Billy suggested.

"Okay," Noelle said.

She and Jonathan changed direction. They all walked into the backyard. When they turned the corner into the corral, Kelly growled.

Noelle was immediately concerned. "What is it, Kelly?"

The fur on Kelly's back stood up straight as she growled again. Suddenly, Lucy burst out of the stable, riding Missy. Lucy was dressed as Santa Claus, and wildly waving the butcher knife, which gleamed in the moonlight.

Kelly ran at her, barking furiously. Noelle yelled, "Kelly, no!"

Jonathan shouted above the din, "It's Lucy!"

Kelly's teeth were bared. She barked, and jumped at Missy's feet. Lucy galloped away with Kelly following. She swung the knife dangerously close to Kelly's head.

Noelle ran up to the barking dog, grabbing her collar, while trying to dodge Lucy.

Billy yelled, "Dad, Joey's gun!"

Jonathan quickly unzipped his overnight bag, and pulled out Joey's gun. He pointed it at Lucy. "Stop, Lucy, or I'll shoot!"

Lucy looked away from Noelle toward Jonathan. In that instant, Noelle pulled Kelly by the collar, and they both ran back toward Jonathan and Billy.

Jonathan carefully advanced on Lucy. She called out to him. "Dear Brother, listen to the song Cousin Santa Claus taught me!"

Jonathan kept the .357 Magnum trained on Lucy. She sang, "Slashing through the snow, In a one horse open sleigh. O'er the fields we go, Slashing all the way! Bells on bobtails ring, Making spirits bright. Oh what fun it is to slash and sing, A slaying song tonight!"

Lucy rode toward Jonathan, the butcher knife ominously whizzing through the air. Jonathan cocked his gun, but before he could shoot, another shot hit Lucy in the back of her shoulder.

She fell off Missy, and Jonathan, Noelle, and Billy ran to Lucy and the horse. Jonathan glanced back at the cabin. Louie stood at the Dutch door, his gun still pointed at the corral.

Jonathan pointed his gun at Louie, and Louie threw down his 9mm. He put up his hands.

"I know I fucked you up, Johnny, but I just shot Lucy to save you, so maybe we could call it quits."

Jonathan sighed, lowering his gun. Lucy moaned, and Noelle ministered to her. "We need to get her inside."

Noelle was the first to enter, opening the door wide. She saw Tommy on the bed, who was awake, and trying to sit up. She ran to him.

"Tommy! Are you okay?"

"I think so. Sorry, I told them where you live."

Noelle hugged him. "I'm just glad you're not dead!"

Louie placed a bloody Lucy on the bed. She slurred drunkenly. "Call the doctor, you idiot!"

"Fuck you, Lucy." Louie walked away disgusted.

"Dominic, call the family's doctor!" Lucy demanded.

Dominic walked over to Louie. "I take orders from Big Louie."

"Somebody give me some fucking wine for this pain!" Lucy shouted.

Noelle snickered. "Interesting problem in chemistry. Sweet wine often turn nice woman sour . . ."

Jonathan laughed. "Confucius?"

"Charlie Chan," Noelle said.

Louie started pacing. "Uncle Vito's gonna be a problem."

Jonathan said, "I've got a feeling Uncle Vito doesn't know about this."

Louie turned to Lucy. "But, Lucy, you told me Uncle Vito wanted Jonathan dead."

"I lied," Lucy said smugly.

Louie became furious. "You bitch! I'll kill you!"

Louie ran at Lucy, his big hands strangling her. Jonathan and Noelle pulled him off of her. Jonathan tried to calm him down. "No, Louie. Uncle Vito will take care of her."

Lucy became circumspect. "Jonathan, we don't have to tell Vito! I fucked up! I'm sorry. I'll never do it again . . . and besides I brought you a present."

Jonathan shook his head in disbelief. "You must be kidding, Lucy! You think we're 10 years old, and you just kicked me?"

"Your present is on the counter."

Jonathan's curiosity was piqued. He walked to the counter, and unwrapped the present. A fifth of vodka. Jonathan took a deep breath, looking at it. He licked his lips.

Billy pleaded, "Don't do it, Dad."

Noelle reached out, touching Billy's shoulder. Jonathan looked at them. He put the bottle down, and walked back to the bed.

"Lucy, why did you want me dead?"

"So I could be *consigliere*. I want that power!"

"You can have the job. I'm through being blackmailed. I'm going to talk to Uncle Vito. After all . . ." Jonathan winked at Noelle. ". . . he is a businessman."

Lucy wasn't worried. "Vito will never believe you."

Louie surprised her. "I'll back up Johnny."

And Jonathan had another surprise. "Thanks, Louie, but I think I've got all the proof I need right here."

Jonathan took the videotape from his bag, and put it in the VCR.

Lucy watched him suspiciously. "What's that?"

Jonathan didn't answer her. He just started the tape. When Lucy recognized the library, she narrowed her eyes, and swallowed nervously. Jonathan fast forwarded, while everyone watched in anticipation.

Lucy appeared on the tape, listening at the door to the surveillance room. Jonathan stopped the tape, backed it up, and played it.

Everyone watched Vito, Martin, and Lucy walk into the surveillance room, and Lucy walk back out alone. They watched her leave the door ajar, and eavesdrop.

Jonathan stopped the tape, smiling triumphantly at the amazed faces. "Lucy, let's get that bullet out of you. I'm gonna set up a very important meeting!"

At dawn the next day, Missy the Mare shook herself awake. Everybody in Noelle's cabin was asleep in their clothes.

Lucy was on the bed. Dominic sat in a chair next to the bed with his chin resting on his chest. He held his gun limply at his side.

Louie slept on the floor, snoring, next to Billy, Kelly, Noelle, and Jonathan. Several blankets covered them and the floor.

Jonathan's eyes opened. He stood, stretching, and Kelly did the same. Jonathan knelt down, and Kelly came to him, licking his face. Jonathan hugged her tightly.

Then Kelly went to Noelle, licking her face until Noelle awakened. "Morning, Kelly girl. Hi, Jonathan."

"Hi, there. I remember you."

"Big day ahead of us. I think it's funny, Tommy was so jazzed by all this action, that he wanted to join the gang. I had to talk him into taking himself home last night."

"Louie said he was a brave kid. I wish courage came in a bottle."

"I wish we had some insurance."

A light bulb went off in Jonathan's head. He grabbed Noelle's face, and kissed her full on the lips.

"You're brilliant! You just gave me a great idea!"

"What is it?"

"Go grab the biggest suitcase you can find, and trust me." Then Jonathan raised his voice, and made an announcement to the sleeping troops.

"Rise and shine. It's Showtime!"

≈

The Rolls Royce pulled up to a security gate of an office building. Jonathan drove. Noelle rode shotgun. Billy was between them.

In the back seat, Lucy and Kelly sat between Louie and Dominic. They were cramped, and Lucy's disdain was clear.

The Guard waved them through. "Morning', Mr. Weber."

Jonathan greeted him warmly. "Happy New Year, Howard."

Jonathan parked in front of the building. He and Noelle got out. Kelly tried to climb over Lucy to follow them.

"Get this fucking dog off of me!" Lucy shouted.

Everybody laughed at Lucy's predicament. Noelle patted the front seat. "Kelly, c'mere. Stay with Billy."

Kelly jumped over the seat, and licked Billy's face. Jonathan smiled. "Lucy, I think you've got enough guards to keep you in line."

"Fuck you, Johnny."

"Fuck you, too, Lucy."

Jonathan carried a big suitcase, and led Noelle down the hall. "Why wasn't the guard suspicious?" she asked.

"The family owns the building."

"Oh . . ." Noelle nodded, impressed. Jonathan unlocked a door with a sign: "Weber, Weber, and Weber, Attorneys at Law."

Jonathan and Noelle entered. Jonathan turned on the lights, and led Noelle to a huge vault. He worked the combination.

Noelle's eyes were like saucers. "Is there money in there?"

Jonathan swung open the heavy door, and walked inside. Noelle followed closed behind. The shelves were lined with cash.

Noelle gasped. "Oh my! Whose money is this?"

"Unlaundered family funds."

"There must be millions here!"

"I figure upwards of 10 million. I'm gonna take five."

"You're gonna steal five million dollars?! The Mob never forgets!"

"This is my insurance. I know my net worth is more than five million. Vito and my father are signers on everything. I can walk away, even if Vito says no."

Jonathan loaded the suitcase with cash. "Start packing."

Noelle grabbed an armful of $10,000 packets of money.

17

Vito's house was a mansion with fountains and magnificent trees. Jonathan drove the Rolls Royce through the security gates.

A Butler ushered Jonathan and his crew across a white marble floor into the library. Jonathan carried the suitcase and the video-tape. Louie held on to a squirming Lucy with his gun pointed into her back.

Everybody entered the library. Martin was already there. Jonathan put down the suit-case, and much to Martin's surprise, Jonathan hugged him hello. When they released, Noelle shook Martin's hand.

Jonathan swallowed the lump in his throat. "Thank you for coming, Father."

"You're welcome, son, but what's this all about? I don't think Vito would want Noelle here. She's not family. And, Lucy, why is your arm in a sling? Louie, put that gun away!"

Jonathan tried to soothe Martin. "Noelle's okay, Father." Jonathan's eyes scanned the walls for a camera. "And, Uncle Vito, if you're listening, Lucy tried to have us killed, said you ordered it, and Louie saved us. I also have a videotape of Lucy eavesdropping on you and Father."

A moment of silence. Martin was worried. Vito came out of another door in the library.

"Louie, put the gun down."

Everyone watched Louie drop his arm to his side. Lucy smiled at Vito. He didn't smile back.

"Lucy, I'll deal with you later . . ."

Lucy's smile changed to terror.

Vito turned to Jonathan. "Hello, Jonathan."

"Hello, Uncle Vito. This is Noelle Splendor."

Vito and Noelle approached each other and shook hands. "How do you do, Ms. Splendor."

"Call me Noelle, Vito."

Vito and Martin raised their eyebrows. Lucy snickered. Louie and Dominic exchanged worried glances.

Jonathan cleared his throat nervously. "Uncle Vito, in the past, I have always asked your permission . . ."

Vito nodded. Jonathan swallowed, taking a deep breath. "This time, I'm not going to."

Martin saw Vito's brows furrow. He tried to stop Jonathan from continuing. "Jonathan, maybe you . . ."

"It's all right, Father. I'm leaving the family business."

"No one leaves alive," Vito said gravely.

"Then kill me now," Jonathan responded, "because I'm walking out that door, and Noelle and Billy are coming with me."

Jonathan extended his hand to Noelle. She took it. They walked toward the door, the suitcase, and Billy. Vito watched them carefully.

Jonathan continued talking. "Lucy wants to be *consigliere*. I want out. You wouldn't let my mother go. She wasn't strong enough to escape. I am."

Vito narrowed his eyes. He looked at Martin for support, but Martin surprised him. "Let him be, Vito. Billy is still Senator Kohler's grandson. It would be good politically to keep that tie alive."

"Literally!" Jonathan said resoundingly.

Vito thought about this. He walked to the bar, and poured himself a drink. "Want a drink, Jonathan?"

"I don't have time, Uncle Vito. There's a sailboat waiting for us."

Vito chuckled. "I find it hard to believe you've changed so quickly . . . that you don't want a drink."

"I didn't say, I didn't want it. I said, I don't have time." Jonathan smiled at Martin. "I'm practicing dying."

Martin laughed, but stopped when Vito stared at him curiously. "My sister used to say that."

Martin nodded. "She taught it to me."

Jonathan said somberly, "Mother was wiser than we thought."

Vito became contemplative. "I never had time for philosophy. My job was working for the family." He sighed deeply. "Jonathan, what's in the suitcase?"

"Five million dollars from the office vault."

Martin is astonished. "What?!"

"You both have access to all my wealth. This is all I want."

Vito understood. "Invest it wisely, Jonathan."

Jonathan smiled broadly. "That means you approve?"

Vito shrugged his shoulders. "Let's just say, I loved my sister. I love you. I wish you and Noelle Splendor contentment."

Noelle laughed. "My kind of guy. Thank you, Vito. Come visit anytime."

Noelle went to him, and shook his hand. Jonathan approached, also to shake Vito's hand, but Vito pulled him closer for a hug. Martin beamed, also hugging Noelle.

As everyone else watched this warm moment, Lucy realized no one was paying attention to her. She abruptly pushed Louie off balance, grabbed his gun, and pulled Billy to her as a hostage. Kelly barked as Louie and Billy yelped.

"Lucy, have you gone mad?!" Martin yelled at her.

Noelle called to Kelly. "Kelly, come here."

Kelly obeyed immediately, coming to Noelle's side.

Lucy spoke cautiously. "I'll be leaving now . . . with the money!"

She yanked up the suitcase, and pulling a terrified Billy with her, she slowly moved into the foyer.

Everyone carefully followed her. Lucy pointed the gun at Billy's head. "Stop following us, or I kill Billy!"

Everyone stopped but Jonathan, who continued toward her. Vito restrained him, and Lucy edged toward the front door.

Vito spoke calmly. "Lucy, I know about the cocaine."

Surprised, Lucy stopped in her tracks. Everyone stared at Vito.

"What are you talking about?" Lucy asked nervously.

"I have my own videotapes. You're out of control, but we can help."

"Your kind of help, I don't want. You know, Uncle Vito, I thought you of all people would understand. You taught us if a partner doesn't agree with you, you kill him. You said, if somebody refuses to come when you call, he's gonna die, even when he didn't do anything else wrong . . . Remember, Christmas Day?"

"What about it?" Vito asked suspiciously.

"You told me to call Jonathan. Have him come see us about the 'Slay Ride' in New York. But he refused to come. He said, get another lawyer."

"I remember," Vito confirmed.

"But, Vito," Martin interrupted. "You had given me your word you wouldn't hurt Jonathan."

"But I didn't give my word!" Lucy shouted gleefully. "Uncle Vito, I thought you would reward me for killing the guy that refused to come when you called, when you weren't in a position to kill him yourself."

"You figured wrong, Lucy . . . about a lot of things. Louie, for example."

Louie and Lucy, both startled, exchanged guilty glances. Vito addressed his nephew.

"Louie, she's been fucking you because she thought you'd be crowned capo one day."

An embarrassed Louie shuffled his feet. "I knew that, Uncle Vito, but at least I was smart enough to be gettin' laid, even if I wasn't smart enough to be a Don."

Lucy rolled her eyes. "You guys make me sick. You're running gambling and loan shark-ing rackets worth $300 million a year, and all you want is to be on top, just so you can get some pussy! Then after you get it, you kill it. Isn't that the way it works, Uncle Vito? Kill all the Suzy Q's when you're done with 'em. Well, this one ain't sticking around!"

Lucy pushed Billy to the front door, and turned her back on the others.

In that instant, Jonathan pulled out Joey's .357 Magnum from inside his belt, and shot Lucy right in the head. Her dead body slumped to the floor. Red blood against white marble.

Billy and Jonathan ran to each other, and Noelle and Kelly joined Jonathan in hugging Billy.

Vito turned to Martin. "We're gettin' too old for this shit . . ."

≈

Noelle steered while Jonathan and Billy fished under a red sky. A bucket of water already had several fish in it.

Billy yelled, "Hook up! Hook up!"

Noelle turned into the wind and slowed the boat down. Billy reeled in a whopper sized fish.

"Wow! What a beauty!"

"Great fish, Billy, but throw it back in," Jonathan said. "The bucket's full."

"But, Dad, it's my biggest catch!" Billy protested.

Noelle intervened. "Set it free, Billy. We've got the rest of our lives to fish . . ."

Billy unhooked the squirming creature, and returned it to the water to reclaim its freedom. Noelle steered the boat so the wind filled the sails.

Jonathan put his rod down, and walked to stand next to Noelle. He put his arm around her shoulders, and kissed her nose.

"Yeah, Billy. We're gonna sleep with the fishes!"

And with that, they sailed away into the sunset . . .

Epilogue

Jimmy and Oleo, are you here?

Always and in all ways.

This was fun. It was fun to fantasize about a new love. I can't help but wonder if I ever really will fall in love again. I don't suppose you're able to predict the future, are you?

No. We engineer things to help create the future, and we whisper ideas into people's brains to help them imagine what can be, so that they can make it a reality, but it is still up to the humans to execute those ideas. You must make the choice every second of every day in your pursuit of happiness.

We have to take responsibility for our own actions and hold others accountable for theirs.

Yes. Life is a merry-go-round and always remember to have gratitude as your mainstay.

My mom told me ever since I was a little girl that whenever I saw someone less fortunate than I, that I was to think, "There but for the Grace of God, go I."

Thank you, God, for the gift of being able to write.

≈

Bestselling author Dr. Audrey J. Levy is a story-teller at heart. It started when she was just 6 years old, spinning tales for her father by turning her weekly spelling words into a cohesive story while sitting in his lap. You are such a great writer, he told her. You're going to be very famous one day, he told her. Sounds idyllic, right? Well. Not so much.

In the years that followed, Audrey witnessed and experienced her father's old-fashioned method of discipline, which was a brief but certainly emphatic whipping with a red belt. His loud, frequent yelling was not music to her family's ears. As an adult, Audrey witnessed and experienced drug abuse, estrangement from her family, disinheritance by her parents, a 20-year union with a now-deceased alcoholic neuropsychologist, an attempted rape by an emotionally disturbed teenage male, and was told of three alleged family suicides, among other things. Pretty much the laundry list of dysfunctional family dynamics and co-dependency.

Despite all that, or perhaps because of all that, she likes to say, Audrey became a licensed Marriage and Family therapist and earned her Doctorate in Psychology. She also pioneered a journal writing method to help herself and others heal old wounds—finding hope, recovery, and redemption.

Audrey has written a dozen screenplays, a novel, multiple novellas, and a stage play. She wrote, produced, and was the lead actress in her fifteen-minute short, "War and Family." Two of Audrey's screenplays made it to the finals of Mr. Steven Spielberg's Chesterfield Writing Competition, and a third screenplay made it to the finals of Mr. Redford's Sundance Competition. She currently lives on a houseboat in California.

Made in the USA
Las Vegas, NV
06 December 2021

36321125R00132